# EVERGREEN

# EVERGREEN

## A Homecoming Like No Other

*Stephanie Galay*

ISBN 978-1-7773608-2-5

# Dedication

This book is for my daughters Sophia and Kalina. Never let anyone tell you can't and when someone tells you can, you definitely should. For my parents, thank you so much for believing in me, your support and encouragement and the kick in the pants to get this off my desk. For my husband who never made me feel like my need to write was taking time away from us and your unique ways of supporting me over the years.

This book is for all the people in the world who don't think they are good enough, who are scared to take a chance, or think they are too old or too busy to chase their dreams. There will never be a better time, you will never feel good enough or brave enough, so just do it. You'll be surprised what you can accomplish when you let yourself go.

Thank you all, so much! We did it.

# Acknowledgements

EVERGREEN is the product of over 20 years of growth, support, and encouragement. There have been so many people involved in this journey, I can't possibly name them all. Below, with family members already thanked in the dedication, are the people who have been major players in getting this book to publication. It has been a long road, and this really wouldn't have happened without each and every one of you.

**Sandra Wickham**, Creative Ink Festival queen. You and the CIF organizing committee pulled me from the shadows and introduced me to a world I can now never leave. I am forever in your debt. I love you all.

**Adam Dreece and Tyner Gillies**. You provided the first unbiased words of praise and encouragement which fuelled me for months and led to first completed draft. Words will never express my gratitude.

**Manny Frishberg**. I cherish the afternoon of conversation that led to the edits you provided with encouraging feedback. EVERGREEN is stronger for your sage advise and words of wisdom.

**Faye Arcand**. Thank you for bringing me into the Kelowna writer's group, for your friendship, and the knowledge you imparted.

Members of the Kelowna Writer's Group (again too many to name all of you). You provided a truly safe place for me to share my work aloud. I thank all of you for your appreciation, support, enthusiasm, and feedback. COVID has me missing our meetings and comradery.

**Jo-Anne (Morefield) Sparrow**, what can I say that I haven't already? Your insights as a reader were invaluable, your love of the story and the characters and your unparalleled (unbiased) excitement for brainstorming important changes really made EVERGREEN what it is today. Thank you, I love you.

**Michelle Caskie** for an amazing job with the original cover art, I already can't wait for the next one.

**Josh Pantellaresco**, for the editing you didn't really want to do and the advice on where and how to start in the pantheon of publishing and marketing. You made it look much less scary.

**Jonas Saul**. Thank you for all the fine tuning at the end, for lifting me up when I was down and shining a light on the end of the tunnel when I had forgotten there was one, for sharing your expertise and for your guidance in the final stages.

I can't tell you enough how much each of you mean to me. This is for all of us.

# Chapter 1

10:53 p.m.

The last of the daylight was gone. My headlights cut swaths out of the darkness to reveal short lengths of yellow lines ahead.

Evergreen was the last place in the world I wanted to be going, but my parents' deaths two days ago left me no choice.

A highway sign seemed to flash in neon as I drove passed. EVERGREEN 56 miles. My chest tightened. I took a few deep breaths and lit a cigarette to relax.

"*Liz, make sure you get here before midnight.*" Shelley's warning echoed in my head as I drove. "*The fog hasn't been deadly since high school, but it still burns.*"

I glanced at the time on my dash.

11:08 p.m.

*Shit, this is going to be close.*

I pressed harder on the gas, and my fingers found the volume on the stereo. The music vibrated through my seat, untangling the knot in my stomach.

The closer I got to my hometown, the faster my memories came. My friends, my parents, the fog that became caustic and deadly after midnight, the real-life nightmare that made me leave in the first place. Five years away hadn't erased a single scar from my soul.

The flat highway started to roll over the foothills that surround my hometown. Patches of mist obscured my view. My foot eased off the pedal to reduce my speed. Clear air diminished, the mist became fog, and the heat of the late summer night was doused. I shivered and traded my open window for the heater.

A slow burn developed in my shoulders and spread into my neck and upper back; I realized I was leaning toward the windshield, a useless attempt to see farther down the road. As I leaned back against my seat, my phone buzzed. My arms jerked at the unexpected sound, and I swerved across the centerline. I corrected my steering, then peeked at the phone mounted on my dash.

A text from Shelley 11:46 p.m.: *It's almost midnight. Where are you?*

I glanced back to the road. The welcome sign was barely visible through the thickening fog. The town limits were within reach, and safety was only a few more minutes away.

A rush of adrenaline burned cold through my veins.

*One more cigarette.*

I drew the smoke deep into my lungs. My heart raced with the flood of nicotine in my blood, then skipped a beat when my phone buzzed again.

Shelley 11:52 p.m.: *SERIOUSLY LIZ WHERE ARE YOU? Eight minutes!*

I wiped my hands on my thighs, one at a time, then swished a sip of water around my mouth to quench the dryness. As I drove under the first streetlights of town, I took a final drag off my cigarette. When I rolled down my window to throw out the butt, the cold dampness of the fog prickled my skin. I closed the window and dropped the butt into my water bottle instead.

Another text from Shelley: 11:55 p.m.: *ARE YOU HERE?*

A minute later, Shelley's apartment building came into view. I activated the hands-free and called her.

"Cutting it a bit close, don't you think?" she asked without so much as a hello.

"I know, I know. Come down and let me in, okay. I'm parking out front."

11:59 p.m. glared at me from the dash as I cut the engine and wrenched my bag from the back seat. I jumped out of my car and bolted across the street. The fog smelled like burnt sugar and rotting oranges and stung my exposed skin, like lime juice over an open wound. Shelley opened the door and let me squeeze through, then pulled hard to force it closed behind me.

Neither of us said a word as we hurried toward the elevator and rode it to the penthouse suite.

Shelley ushered me through her door, then closed and locked it behind us. Before I could move toward the hall, she grabbed me in a firm hug.

"Ugh, take it easy …"

Shelley loosened her grip.

"You're my best friend, and I haven't seen you in forever." She unwrapped her arms but kept a hold of me. "Not to mention that you scared the hell out of me tonight." Her green eyes mirrored the concern in her voice.

Shelley dropped her hands to her hips, and I put down my bag. I rubbed at my forearms. They no longer hurt, but the exposure to the midnight fog had left my skin red and irritated.

"I'm sorry. I knew the timing would be tight, but I felt like I needed to get here tonight. I needed a familiar face, a real friend. You know?" The threat of tears increased with each word.

Shelley's posture softened. She nodded and flipped her long, blond hair over her shoulder. She took my bag and gestured toward the great room at the end of the short hallway.

"Why don't you go sit down? I'll take this to your room." Her voice was quiet and soothing as Shelley scooted past me and turned down the corridor I assumed led to the bedrooms.

I wandered past the open kitchen and into the living room, surveying the space as I crossed to the sofa. A bar top counter separated the kitchen from the living room, and high ceilings made the ample space feel even bigger. Behind the couch, a picture window offered an expansive view over the park, now shrouded in the dense fog that blanketed the entire town. Not even the streetlights were getting through now, so I closed the drapes and sank into the oversized sofa.

I pulled the elastic out of my hair and ran my fingers through the wavy, light brown mess. Shelley returned with two glasses of wine. She handed one to me, then took a sip from hers before sitting beside me with one foot tucked up under her athletic frame.

EVERGREEN

"I've missed you, Liz."

"I've missed you, too."

"Have you gotten any more information about your parents' accident?"

"Nothing more than we already knew, and none of that makes any sense. There were no other cars involved, the road conditions were favorable, and as far as they can tell, the car was mechanically sound. So, I don't know." I traced along the rim of the glass with my finger. "It's like they ran into an invisible wall or something."

When I raised my glass to my lips, light glinted off the moisture in my friend's eyes.

"I can't believe they're gone." Shelley's voice cracked. "I just had dinner with them a week ago."

"They loved you. Mom always referred to you as my sister, even when we were kids. I think she wished you were."

Shelley reached a hand toward my knee but diverted when her phone rang. She answered it before I could glimpse the name on the screen.

"Yes, she made it. She couldn't have cut it any closer if she had meant to, though." Shelley paused, listening to the person on the other end. "Okay, I'll tell her. Talk to you later." She set her cell phone on the coffee table. "It was Jack. He wanted to make sure you made it okay."

I downed my wine in a series of quick gulps. The sound of his name wound my stomach into a knot and made my heart race.

"More wine?" I went to the kitchen to retrieve the bottle without waiting for her response.

5

"Have you talked to anyone since you left?" Shelley asked.

Shelley's glass didn't require much of a top-up, but I poured into both glasses anyway, then put the bottle on the table as I reclaimed my spot on the sofa.

"No. I was trying to forget Evergreen. Remember? Talking to any of them would have defeated the purpose."

"But you talk to me all the time."

"Yeah, but that's different. You're more like a sister than a friend. I still talk … *was* still talking to Mom and Dad all the time." My voice softened as I corrected myself—the moisture of tears built at the corners of my eyes.

"Well, I thought it might be nice to have the others come back here after the funeral, a private thing, just for the inner circle. I know Dee and the guys will get together after anyway, so it might as well be here."

The thought of seeing the friends I had left behind tied my stomach in knots.

"Yeah, sure, if you want." I shrugged. "But I'm not so sure any of them will be happy to have me there." I pulled my knees to my chest and wrapped one arm around them. "They all loved Mom and Dad. I'm sure they're mourning as much as I am."

"Yes, we're all grieving, Liz, which is why we should all be together. No, not everyone is super pleased with you, but we're adults. I would hope Jack and Deanna would be able to put their feelings aside for one night."

"I suppose you're right. You know them better than I do now, so if you think it will be okay, then I trust you." I covered a yawn with my free hand.

Our conversation shifted to lighter topics, and my second glass of wine emptied at a much more reasonable pace.

A short time after she set the empty bottle on the table, Shelley opened her mouth and was unable to cover a yawn of her own. She reached over and pushed a button on her phone. The screen came to life.

"No wonder we're yawning. It's nearly one a.m."

"That explains it." I tipped my head back and let the last of my wine drain into my mouth. Shelley, not wanting to waste any wine, followed suit. We set our empty glasses next to the bottle. Shelley stood and extended a hand to pull me up.

"Come on. I'll show you your room."

She led me down the hall to the first door on the right. She flicked on the light as we entered the space.

"No closet, but feel free to unpack and put your stuff in the armoire. You have a bathroom, and you don't need to worry about flushing or using hot water. Each faucet in this place has a temperature control on it."

"Thank you, Shelley." I embraced her almost as tight as she had hugged me, but I let her go much sooner.

"Have a good sleep, sis." Shelley winked, then started for the door. "I'm at the end of the hall if you need anything."

I rummaged through my bag for PJs and Ibuprofen. Once changed and medicated, I climbed into the enormous bed. I smiled to myself while waiting for sleep to take me.

Shelley reminded me of happier times. I closed my eyes and let the memories take over. It didn't take long for them to weave their way to Jack.

Friends since kindergarten, we started dating the summer after junior high. We never fought, except for the day I told him goodbye. One dark thought led to another while I drifted off to sleep.

*My friends and I stood scattered across the meadow just beyond my parents' property. Thick clouds made the mid-afternoon sky darker than usual, and the electricity in the air signaled an approaching storm. Plumes of breath were visible from each of us in the cold February air.*

*Shelley spun around to face me. "Where did it go?"*

*"I don't know, I don't know!" I spun around and glimpsed the demon as it reappeared behind Shelley.*

*"Look out." My warning gave her just enough time to duck.*

*The towering red creature swung at Shelley and missed, clipping Kevin in the head instead. He flew through the air and landed fifteen feet away. Dave ran to his brother's side to assess the damage.*

*"He's out cold."*

*Stacey put gloved fingers to her temples and shut her eyes tight. A huge rock rose out of the snow behind our enemy and hurtled through the air. A thunderous crack sounded as the stone impacted its target. The demon roared and lurched forward, but somehow kept its balance. It turned and moved toward Stacey, eyes glowing blue. In two giant strides, it closed the*

8

*distance. With one fluid movement, it grabbed Stacey by the throat, squeezed, and tossed her aside like an empty pop can.*

*Deanna screamed as her twin's lifeless body hit the ground. She ran to her sister and sank to her knees. She hung her head for a moment, then tilted it skyward. Her scream turned guttural, and the ground beneath the demon shook. It lost its footing and stumbled backward.*

*Jack and Shelley charged from behind; homemade weapons held high. I ran to help, glancing at Deanna and Stacey as I passed them. The sound of the earth's rumble rose to a deafening roar. I kept running toward the source but couldn't take my eyes off Stacey's lifeless body.*

*"Liz, STOP!" Shelley's voice broke my stare. I skidded to a halt, my focus now on the demon. It staggered forward and fell at my feet. It glowered at me, eyes now dim with the last of its life, and plunged a gnarled appendage into my chest.*

I sat up in bed, clutching the blankets to my heaving chest. I couldn't remember having a single dream in the five years since I left Evergreen. Now I was glad I hadn't. I stared into the gray light of the pre-dawn morning and tried to catch my breath. With shaking hands, I drank the glass of water on the bedside table, then went to the bathroom to refill it.

I placed my hands on the counter and hung my head with my eyes closed. I needed any memory other than the one that had come in dream form. When I opened my eyes and lifted my head, my gaze found the scar beneath my left shoulder. I had never had any pain with the wound, even as the demon plunged part of itself into me. Now the scar throbbed in time with my heartbeat.

*Weird. Must be left over from the dream.* I rubbed my hand over the scar, trying to soothe the sensation.

As I made my way back to bed, I noticed a book sitting on the vanity. I paused for a second, not able to recall if it had been there earlier. When I was close enough to reach it, I recognized it without having to pick it up. The soft, embossed cover gave away its identity—one of our journals from senior year.

"Why the hell would she put that here?" I opted to leave it where it sat. One nightmare was already more than I had wanted for one night.

# Chapter 2

I rolled over. A bolt of pain ripped through my left shoulder, where I had been stabbed almost six years ago in a battle for my life. I rubbed the spot and recalled the nightmare. A shiver ran down my spine. Maybe the throbbing the night before hadn't been part of my dream.

Before I could get out of bed, the door opened after a light knock.

"Oh, good, you're awake." Shelley let herself in and sat down on the bed beside me. "Want to go to the diner for breakfast?"

"How are you always so perky in the morning? Especially after so much wine?" I rubbed a hand over my scar.

"Ibuprofen, and a lot of water before I climb into bed. That, and I'm a morning person. You should know that by now."

"I was hoping you had grown out of it."

"So, breakfast? The diner?"

My stomach rumbled. I glanced down and crossed my arms over it.

"Yeah, sounds great. Can I shower before, or do I have to wait till after?"

"I think after. I need coffee and bacon, stat!"

The diner was the best place in this small town for breakfast and was only a couple of blocks from Shelley's apartment, so we opted to walk.

The mid-August morning was already heating up. Delighted laughter of children playing in the park across the street filled the air. Huge weeping willows stood sentinel while their dangling, leaf-filled branches swept across the grass in the morning breeze.

When we entered, I was embraced by the sweet aromas of home-baked bread and the nutty richness of freshly brewed coffee. I closed my eyes and inhaled deeply to take it all in.

"Hey, Shelley, over here." Dave said.

I turned at the sound of the familiar voice to see Dave Henderson waving. Kevin, his younger brother, sat next to him. I took a deliberate, steadying breath and wiped my palms on my denim-covered hips before we started toward their table.

"Hey, Liz." Kevin stood and threw his massive arms around me, lifting me off the ground in a huge bear hug. He kissed my forehead like he always had, then set me back on my feet.

"It's good to see you haven't changed, Kev." I took the seat next to Shelley, who had sat quickly to avoid a bear hug of her own.

I glanced across the table to the smaller, more subdued brother. "Hi, Dave, it's been a long time."

The waitress came a moment later with coffee cups for Shelley and me in one hand, and a pot of black magic in the other. After filling our cups, she topped up Dave and Kevin's, then took our breakfast orders, and scurried away.

"We were so sorry to hear about your parents, Liz," Dave said before taking a sip of his coffee. "The news of their car accident took us all by surprise."

"Thanks, Dave, I appreciate it." I stared at my cup to hide the tears. Once again, subtlety was not my strength. Dave reached over and squeezed my hand. A tear dropped into the steaming black liquid in my cup. A small, nervous laugh followed, and I raised my head to see the smirks on my friends' faces. I wiped away the few tears that dared to follow, which prompted another short, self-conscious laugh—time to divert attention. I took a breath and straightened up.

"So, what have you guys been up to lately?"

"I've got a contracting business which keeps me busy." Dave stirred his coffee. "Business is good. There are lots of new houses going up. It seems like city people want to escape the rush but still want a home close enough to commute into Denver. Evergreen is the perfect location."

"That's good for the town, I guess," I said.

"I try to source local materials as much as possible. The Mitchells' hardware store has been able to supply most of what we need for the majority of the builds."

Kevin stopped pouring sugar into his coffee. "I get an extra paycheck working for him when I'm not on call for the fire department."

"How often is that?" I asked.

"Right now, rescue calls happen more often than I'd like, a lot of car—" He stopped short. "Sorry, Liz."

I shook my head. "It's okay. Those are the calls you get. You don't need to apologize."

"Well, anyway, the last couple winters Dave's kept me solvent and in great shape." Kevin flexed and pressed his fingers into his biceps. "Rock solid."

The waitress came with our food, ending Kevin's display, but she smiled at him, and I noticed his wink in return.

Being with the Henderson brothers felt like I had never left. The conversation was comfortable and light, never feeling forced or awkward. Part of me wished this moment could last forever but being with my friends meant I could never forget what had happened to us. The truth was ugly, and one I couldn't escape. We had watched Stacey die in front of us. It was a close call for Kevin and me, too. I had worked hard to put the nightmare behind me and didn't want to think of it now.

Forty minutes later, we were in the parking lot.

"Liz, pass me your phone." I handed it to Dave and watched as he entered his number. "If you need anything, you call me. Got it? Doesn't matter what it is."

"Thanks, Dave." The exchange let me dodge another bear hug from Kevin. This time it was Shelley's turn.

"That goes double for me." Kevin intercepted my phone as Dave attempted to hand it back to me. I reached for it when he had entered his number and found myself pulled into the missed hug. I didn't mind the kiss on the forehead.

EVERGREEN

Back at Shelley's, I put my hair up for a shower and noticed the scar below my left shoulder was pink and puffy as if still healing from a recent wound.

*I must've been scratching at it.*

I stepped under the running water and stayed under its soothing heat longer than needed. I turned off the water, though I could've stayed under it forever, and wrapped myself in a fluffy oversized towel, letting the air dry the rest of me.

Dressed and refreshed from my shower, I went to the picture window in the living room. I contemplated the range of color and activity in the park below. The shroud of fog the night before seemed surreal in comparison. I stepped through the open sliding door to the sprawling balcony and sat cross-legged in a large wicker chair next to Shelley.

I lit a cigarette and let the warmth of the sun wrap itself around me while we sat and watched the kids playing in the park across the street. I found unexpected comfort in the waves of laughter that landed on my ears, bringing memories of my childhood with them.

My heart ached from the recent loss of my parents. It still didn't feel real.

"What do you need to do today?"

I swallowed against the ache in my throat and sniffled back the tickle in my nose before my emotions could take hold. I kept my gaze fixed on the park. I took a final drag before I answered.

"I talked to the lawyer yesterday. I'm meeting with him on Monday. He suggested I go out to the house and check on things, so I guess I'll start there."

"Are you ready for that?"

"No, but I don't think I ever will be."

***

My stomach twisted up not far out of town, and I was silent for most of the drive. When my parents' house came into view, I spoke for the first time since leaving Shelley's.

"It looks the same." I stared at the house and chewed on the side of my thumb, as Shelley parked a short distance from the spot my mom's CRV should have occupied.

"Your parents were always great about maintaining this place." Shelley rested a hand on my shoulder. "And it's only been a few days." Her voice was so soft, I wasn't sure she'd spoken.

With my mom's car missing, it took me a minute to process the fact they weren't just out. Her SUV would never be here again. I tried to clear my throat, but the lump's grip tightened, and the knot in my stomach changed to ice.

"Are you ready?" Shelley nodded toward the house.

I wasn't, but I stepped out of Shelley's vehicle and took in the familiar landscape before fully committing myself. The large, two-story house appeared to have a fresh coat of paint, and the deck seemed clean and free of debris. Baskets hung above the porch that wrapped the house like a skirt. The flower beds surrounding the house looked as I expected for this time of year. They were trimmed, and when I got closer, I noticed a visible lack of deadheads, something possible only with near-constant maintenance.

I raised a hand to my lips to hold back a tearful wail as I realized these flowers were the last my mom would ever plant. I wiped at the tears that managed to escape, hoping Shelley wouldn't notice. A gentle hand on my back told me I wasn't that subtle.

"I don't know if I can do this." I faced Shelley.

"I know it won't be easy, but I'm with you every step of the way. It's all on your pace, okay?"

"Thanks for being here." I smiled through teary eyes. How she didn't hate me for leaving her in this town, I'll never know.

The keys rattled in my trembling hands with each step up to the porch. The nervous knot tried to rise out of my stomach. I stopped at the top as if a wall had sprung up in front of me.

Shelley put a hand on my shoulder. "It's okay, Liz, we'll do this together, one step at a time."

I lowered my head and stared at my feet. "I'm so glad you're here. There's no way I could do this on my own." The shakiness of my voice matched the trembling of my hands.

"It's okay." Shelley stood close to me. "When you're ready."

"It's weird, knowing they won't be in there waiting for me." I hesitated then and extended a hand. "Here, you do it." I handed Shelley the keys and waited for her to move again. She crossed the porch, slipped the key into the lock, and opened the door to my childhood home.

I saw past her into the house. I had forgotten how bright it was. Large windows hung in every wall, letting light spill in from all sides. I took a deep breath and followed Shelley into the living room.

Memories filled every corner of the expansive room. I ran my hand along the arm of the couch, where I'd curled up to read on winter afternoons. I stepped behind my mom's recliner and trailed my fingers on the fabric. In a basket beside the chair, a pair of knitting needles held a project that would never be completed. I closed my eyes, and I could see my mom's eyes twinkle with laughter, and almost smell the hint of coconut oil she put in her hair.

My chest tightened, and the lump in my throat made it hurt to swallow. The tears I fought to hold back spilled down my cheeks in a torrent. Somehow, I found my way to the front of the chair and slumped down with my face in my hands, my body heaving. It was the first time my grief overpowered shock since I'd heard about my parents' car accident three days before.

It felt like forever, but eventually the sobs weakened, and my lungs allowed normal breaths. I blew my nose to open another airway.

"I didn't know you were part goose." Shelley snorted, which caused us both to laugh. We eyed each other, and our chuckles grew into belly laughs.

"Thank you," I panted and held my aching stomach. "I needed that." When I had caught my breath, I stood and offered a hand to Shelley and pulled her off the floor.

With our composure regained, we moved through the house to make sure it was secure.

"We should probably empty the fridge," Shelley said when we entered the kitchen.

"You're right." I turned and considered the large white appliance. Several photos covered a good portion of the top door. I moved closer to get a better look at them and found most were from the last time Mom and Dad had visited me in Topeka. It had only been about six weeks ago, and the still vivid memories danced in my mind. Without thinking, I opened the fridge door, surprised for some reason to find it quite full.

"Can you go out to the garage and see if there is a cooler out there? We might as well take what we can back to your place."

I stared at the contents; my mind unable to recognize any of what I was seeing.

"Are you waiting for penguins to show up?"

I jolted, my hand coming free of the handle on the door. It slammed shut. I heard jars and bottles clang inside from the force of it. "What? No."

"What did you see in there? Anything worth taking?"

"No. Maybe." I scratched my head. "Honestly, I'm not sure. I must have zoned out."

Shelley set the cooler on the floor. "Why don't we check the rest of the house, then we can go through the fridge before we leave."

"Good idea. No sense putting cold stuff into a warm cooler any sooner than necessary."

Shelley checked the kitchen door while I closed and locked the windows, then we went upstairs.

The door to my childhood bedroom stood open. I leaned against the door jam and stared at the trinkets and posters of my youth. They were familiar but somehow seemed unconnected to me now. It was as though I was looking at a stranger's room.

Shelley scooted past me. "Remember how much fun we had in here?" She leaned over my desk, toward the mirror that hung on the wall. "Wow, I haven't seen this in a long time. We look so young." She removed a picture, held in place by its corner tucked behind the mirror.

I padded over and peeked at the picture over her shoulder. She offered it to me for a better look.

*And much more innocent.*

Shelley sat on the stool and poked around. "Our junior year-end barbecue at the lake."

I continued to focus on the picture and let my mind return to the day while she spoke.

It had been a perfect summer day. Bright, sunny, and warm, but not hot. The school year had just finished. My friends and I were celebrating the way we had since grade school, a big party at the lake, followed by a bonfire. In our younger years, our parents had joined us, but this year it was just us. At sixteen and out of junior high, we weren't kids anymore, at least we didn't think so. It had been a true celebration.

The picture drew me further into the recollection. No longer in my childhood bedroom, the memory played like a movie and took on a life of its own. My ears filled with squeals of excitement and raucous laughter from my friends while some played in the water, and others warmed themselves on the beach.

At sunset, we lit the bonfire. When the air cooled, people donned sweaters and swapped shorts for pants. I headed for the parking lot to grab my hoodie, alone for the first time that day. When I heard footsteps crunching on the gravel behind me, I spun and saw Jack.

"I thought you might like some company … it's pretty dark over here."

"I'm glad you caught up with me. It's so quiet, almost too quiet. It's creepy." We got to the car, and I grabbed my bag, so I didn't have to come back to the car again. I pulled out my sweater and set my bag on the ground. Jack picked it up and slung it over his shoulder.

"So, um." He hung his head and kicked a rock with the toe of his shoe while he waited for me to put on my hoodie. "I need your advice on something." He straightened, squared his shoulders, and pushed his hair back out of his face.

"Of course." I slid my hands into my back pockets. "Is everything okay? You seem tense."

"Well, there's a girl I've been friends with for a long time, but I'm not happy being just friends anymore." He kicked another rock and glanced toward the beach. "I'm just not sure if she feels the same way about me. Got any suggestions?"

"Why don't you just tell her how you feel?"

"Well, I thought of that, but what if she doesn't feel the same?" His voice was steeped with tension.

"What if she does? I think you should take the chance. You'll never know if you don't ask, and you might regret not asking someday."

We strolled toward the beach in silence. At the edge of the firelight, Jack stopped short and grabbed my hand. I lurched, one leg kicked up and spun me around to face him. Jack caught me before I could fall forward. When I was still, he stared into my eyes. The dim light from the distant fire made the brilliant blue of his eyes shine as I'd never seen before. My heart fluttered; my cheeks warmed. Something deep within me stirred.

Jack stepped in closer. The space between us melted away. Before I realized what was happening, his lips were on mine. The world around us disappeared. My eyes closed, and I was kissing him back. My entire body tingled, and my heart pounded so hard, I was sure he must be able to hear it. He broke away, and his blue eyes seared into my soul.

"I'm in love with you, Liz," he breathed. "I think I've loved you since kindergarten." I couldn't do anything but nod in agreement. It was as if he had reached into my heart and found feelings I didn't even realize I had.

Jack grabbed me by the waist and kissed me again, then wrapped his arm around my shoulder to guide me back to the party. He smiled at me, and this time I leaned in for a kiss before he could start walking.

When Jack pulled away this time, he grabbed my hand. "We should get back. I think I smell hot dogs and marshmallows." We strolled back to the fire hand in hand.

"Earth to Liz." Shelley's voice shattered my reverie. "Did you hear me?"

"What? No, sorry." I blinked and shook my head, then shifted my attention to her. "What did you say?"

"Where were you just now?"

"I was thinking about the bonfire. It was a perfect day."

"We had lots of perfect days, Liz."

"Yeah, I'm sure we did, but it's hard to remember much of anything past the bad. I don't know how you stay here, constantly reminded of it all." I tossed the photo onto the desk. I glanced around my room and then fixed my gaze on Shelley. "Can we get out of here?"

"Sure, I know this can't be easy for you. We'll go back to my place and have a drink."

The drive back to Shelley's was as quiet as the trip out had been. I was lost in thought and memory. Shelley, I guessed, was quiet for the same reason.

I sank into one of the balcony chairs and set my drink on the table between us. "It was nice to see Dave and Kevin this morning."

"I'm glad you got to see the brothers first. I think they understood the most, why you left like you did. Deanna and Jack didn't take it so well."

"Do they hate me?"

"I know Jack doesn't, and I don't think Dee does either, but her and I don't talk about you. We had a big argument a few years ago, so we decided you were off the table. Jack, on the other hand, asks about you all the time. I'm pretty sure there are still feelings there, but it took him a long time to come to grips with the fact you weren't coming back."

"Any idea what Dee's issue is? Maybe I should go see her and try to talk to her before the funeral."

Shelley tucked a loose strand of hair behind her ear. She took a deep breath and exhaled a heavy sigh, then locked her gaze at the floor.

"She blames you for Stacey's death. Or at least she did. As I said, we don't talk about you, so I don't know how she feels now. You might want to let her make the first move. You know how she can be."

"She's the last person I want mad at me. Remember what her and Stacey did when that asshole was hitting on Stacey at the rink that night? I think we were only in tenth grade."

"Yeah." Shelley let out a soft chuckle. "They worked him over pretty good. I've never seen anyone run from two teenage girls as fast as he did that night."

We both laughed as we remembered the embarrassment on the guy's face. The best part was, neither Deanna nor Stacey had laid a hand on him.

"Maybe you're right. If Dee is pissed at me, maybe I should just let her come to me."

# Chapter 3

Shelley and I stepped out of the car in front of the lawyer's office. The brisk morning air smelled of dew, and the cooler temperature whispered that fall was just around the corner.

"What's this meeting with the lawyer about?"

"I think it's just all the things I need to do before the funeral." I waved my arm above my head. "Only child over here, so automatic executor, and who knows what else." I huffed out a heavy breath. "God, I'd rather be anywhere than here."

We stepped through the door into a spacious reception area. The simplicity of the pine furniture and modern décor was unexpected, and the anxious knot in my stomach started to relax.

I gave my name to the receptionist, my voice shaking, then moved toward the beige sofa, which made up the waiting area.

Shelley pointed to the painting on the wall before I could sit down. "I know that name. I think we went to high school with the artist."

"Wow. It's nice to see local art on the walls."

Shelley sat next to me and ran her fingers through her hair. Neither of us spoke until a few minutes later when a man who appeared to be in his thirties came out and called us into his office.

"Hello, Miss Porter, I'm Harry Matthews."

"Hi." I gestured to my left. "This is my friend, Shelley Nicholls."

He shook hands with each of us, then led us through the etched glass door and closed it behind us.

Four leather armchairs made up a small seating area in front of a desk, which sat close to the wall opposite the door. A law degree, admission to the bar and a business license hung, in matching frames, centered on the wall behind the desk.

I was surprised at how young he appeared to be as the lawyer pointed to the leather chairs. He joined us after picking up the legal pad and a pen from his small desk.

"How are you holding up?" There was genuine concern in his voice.

"It's been a rough few days." I rubbed my hands together, just above my lap.

"I imagine it has been. It's so unfortunate to lose both parents at once. I'm aware you don't have any family in town," he nodded toward Shelley, "but it looks like you have some good support."

"Yes, Shelley's like a sister to me. I'm staying with her while I'm here."

"Good. It's important to have people around you during times like this. There's a lot to do, and if you have someone who can help with the little things and some of the big decisions, it's much easier to bear."

There was a quiet knock, then the door opened. The receptionist entered and set a pitcher of water on the credenza I hadn't noticed when we came in. She left without a word, then returned a moment later with two carafes. I assumed one to be coffee and the other to be hot water. She left just as quickly and closed the door behind her.

"Something for all tastes. Please, ladies, help yourselves."

"Thank you. I'm okay for now."

Shelley, never the shy one, helped herself to a cup of coffee.

"Let's get started then."

He explained what the law would require over the next few days. Several of the tasks, including the funeral arrangements, had options for when and how they were to be completed. Mr. Matthews stopped after each requirement to see if I had questions, then carried on.

At some point, his voice became a rhythmic string of nonsensical words I couldn't understand. Images of my parents lying in coffins swam through my head. I couldn't move. My brain kicked into overdrive and produced an advance screening of their funeral and all it entailed. I closed my eyes and shook my head to clear the images. I couldn't focus.

I blinked a couple of times, then realized he was trying to hand me a glass of water.

"Your eyes glazed over for a bit, there." He set the glass beside me. "Do you want to take a break?"

"No, thank you. It's just, I keep seeing them in caskets. So still, and quiet. So … so …" I wiped an errant tear. "I can't believe they're gone."

"I think we've covered enough for today. Why don't you go back to your friend's place and get some rest? We can set up another meeting to go over the estate after the funeral, or whatever you decide. Everything we've covered is in this package." He handed me a folder with several pamphlets and other papers in it.

"Thank you, Mr. Matthews." I handed him my empty glass. "I appreciate your time. I had no idea where to begin."

Shelley and I left with a long to-do list. That afternoon, we started to tackle it. Our first stop was the funeral home.

We were greeted in the parlor by a middle-aged woman with long, dark hair, which hung in a braid over one shoulder. Her black sheath dress was respectful, but not uptight.

"Hi, my name's Shelley." She pointed at me. "This is my friend, Liz Porter. We need to make some arrangements for her parents."

"It's nice to meet you both. I'm Sarah. Mr. Matthews called a little while ago and told me to expect you. Please, follow me."

The woman led us down a corridor toward the back of the building, her flat shoes padding softly along the carpet. When we reached her office, she moved aside and gestured for us to go in and sit down. She followed and picked up a folder before sitting in the empty chair on our side of the desk as the lawyer had.

"I am sorry for your loss. I can't imagine what you must be going through, losing both your parents at once."

"Thank you." I held my hands together in my lap and rubbed the back of my hand with my thumb.

"Your parents made arrangements with us several years ago. Their wishes are noted here." She handed me the folder. "The expenses have been settled. We just need you to select a date, or dates, for when you'd like the services and burials."

A familiar ache took hold in my throat, and imminent tears stung my eyes. I couldn't speak. I grabbed one of Shelley's hands and squeezed.

"I think one date, as soon as possible." Shelley's voice was soft and calm.

Sarah stood and rounded the desk. She picked up a notebook and pen, then sat back in her chair. She opened the book and flipped a couple of pages.

"We are available this Thursday."

I nodded.

"Would you like the service held here in the building or up at the burial site on the hill?"

I opened my mouth to respond, but my voice was still absent. I looked at Shelley and mouthed the words *on the hill*. She nodded and relayed my decision.

Sarah told us she would be overseeing the preparations, then showed us back to the entrance.

"Again, Miss Porter, I am deeply sorry for your loss. If I may, just one piece of advice. Make sure to stay hydrated, eat, and get plenty of rest over the next few weeks. Grief takes a lot of energy. If you aren't rested, you will be extremely vulnerable to external forces."

"Thank you, Sarah." We started for the parking lot as the door shut behind us.

"That was weird. What do you think she meant by external forces?" Shelley asked when we got to the car.

"I don't know. Probably nothing. She's old, Shelley. Old people talk like that."

\*\*\*

We spent the next couple of days drafting the obituaries, placing the necessary ads in the papers, and going through the rest of the list from the lawyer.

The night before the funeral, Shelley and I watched a movie to take our minds off the dismal tasks of the week. During a commercial break, the local news preview mentioned a story about Evergreen's fog. I perked up when I heard the word.

"What about the fog?"

Shelley peered up from her phone.

"I'm not sure. I wasn't paying attention. I guess we'll have to watch the news before we go to bed."

A while later, Shelley tapped my foot. I jumped, startled by her touch, and opened my eyes.

"Hey, it's on."

I yawned and stretched out of the ball I was in, then extracted myself from the corner of the couch.

"The fog which has blanketed Evergreen nightly for the past several years has once again caused an injury. More with this story is Sage Bristol."

"Thank you, Peter. I'm at the urgent care center in Evergreen, and though details are still scarce, it seems people are being treated for burns, similar to those seen almost six years ago. There have only been a few incidents of burns associated with the fog in the last few years, but things have changed in recent weeks. Before, we had reports of injuries only by people who ventured out after midnight, but now the time of night doesn't seem to matter. Doctors are reporting people attending local urgent care centers and Denver area hospitals with burns they've received well before midnight. We will be following this story as we try to determine why the fog seems to be getting more dangerous. Back to you, Peter."

"Thank you, Sage. The cause of the fog, and its propensity to cause injury, were studied by scientists from all over the country when it first appeared five years ago. No findings have ever been released."

Shelley clicked off the TV and sat facing the blank screen. "I haven't heard of anyone being burned for a long time."

I rubbed at the goosebumps that had risen up on my arms. "Why do you think that's changed?"

"No idea, but I remember when they put the curfew in place, the number of burn victims decreased to almost zero. I think the only incidents since then are people who were stupid enough to stay out late."

"Did you know there had been scientists here back then?" I said. "I sure as hell didn't."

"No, but we were a bit preoccupied," Shelley replied.

"You don't think it could be back, do you?"

"No." She shook her head. "No way. We killed it. We all saw the demon die, literally disappear, right after it stabbed you."

"So why didn't the fog ever go away? I know it still burns." I touched my arm where it had been affected the night I arrived. "But if we killed it …" I glanced toward the dark window. "And if no reason for the fog, or why it burns, was ever determined, what if the fog is connected somehow?"

"I don't know, Liz. That seems like a bit of a stretch. The fog started before that thing showed up. It's much more likely there's some kind of government or military experiment responsible for it. That's probably why there were never any studies or findings released. If the government is involved, they are going to want to keep that wrapped up tight."

"You're probably right. I guess being back here has me a bit paranoid." I drew the back of my hand to my mouth to cover a yawn.

"Liz, you're exhausted. Why don't you go to bed? I can give you something to help you sleep if you want. Tomorrow will be easier if you're rested."

"Thanks, Shelley. A little help can't hurt." I followed her to the bathroom and took the pill she offered. It didn't take long for it to take effect. Within minutes of getting into bed and closing my eyes, images in my mind swirled together. Colors layered and blended together until there was just the endless black of oblivion.

I woke up early the next morning, feeling hungover from the sleeping pill. I was both disappointed and pleased to find it was only six-thirty. I was wide awake and knew I wouldn't be able to fall back asleep, but I was glad I had a few hours for the fog in my head to clear.

# EVERGREEN

I lay in bed for a while, trying not to think about how the day would play out, but the thoughts came, and tears rolled down the sides of my face onto my pillow. I let them flow in hopes I might be able to contain them later. It had been over a week since I had received the news of the fatal crash, and I still couldn't believe it.

Investigators had ruled it a freak accident with no discernible cause. Something had to have happened to cause the driver to swerve. They weren't sure if it had been my mom or dad driving, but there was nothing to indicate what might have occurred. They admitted to pure speculation.

An hour later, I convinced myself to get out of bed and have a shower. Continuing to lie there and dwell wasn't going to end this day any faster.

I took my time under the hot water, letting it soothe me as much as possible before washing. By the time I was dressed, it was close to eight-thirty.

Shelley greeted me in the kitchen, still in her pajamas. She handed me a cup of coffee and offered a shot of whiskey to go with it.

I shook my head. "Thanks, I'll pass for now. I'm sure I'll need a few later, though."

A black Town Car from the funeral home came for us at ten-thirty. We stepped out of the cool of the apartment building into the warmth of the sunny August morning. The cloudless, blue sky issued a silent promise that the weather would hold for the outdoor proceedings.

The driver stood at the back passenger door and opened it as we approached. He offered his condolences as Shelley and I climbed in.

I stared out the window and watched the rest of the world carry on as we drove—children on bikes, love-struck teens walking hand in hand. I envied them. They had families, futures, and lives likely untouched by loss or evil.

When we reached the cemetery, the car followed the road to the top of the cemetery property and stopped in a spot with a spectacular lake view.

The driver cut the ignition and hurried to the back of the car to open my door while I was still undoing my seat belt.

I stepped out of the car and breathed in the fragrance of the abundant flowers which grew throughout the manicured landscape. I closed my eyes, tilted my head back, and inhaled deeply. The floral aroma and the warmth of the sun transported me to a place of tranquility. All too soon, I felt the soft pressure of a hand on my shoulder and opened my eyes. It was time to move on.

Shelley and I followed the stone path to the gravesite. Two gleaming mahogany caskets sat next to each other on rails. My stomach dropped, and my chest tightened. I closed my eyes and shook my head. This couldn't be real. A hand wrapped around mine.

*Shelley.*

I let my eyes open and take in the scene. The funeral director arrived a few moments later and explained the proceedings so I would know what to expect.

Kevin and Dave came into view as Sarah finished her explanation. She handed Shelley and me each a basket filled with white roses.

"How are you holding up?" Kevin hugged me much more gently than I expected, but the kiss on my forehead followed as usual.

What composure I had left broke at the tenderness of his action, and my throat closed up. I swallowed what felt like razor blades and found myself unable to speak. I gave a sideways shrug in response and reached into my pocket for a tissue. I dabbed beneath my dark sunglasses at the corners of my eyes to dry the tears that hadn't had a chance to escape.

"I'm so sorry, Liz. We're here for you." Dave's voice cracked as he spoke. "Whatever you need."

I did my best to smile. The brothers split up and stood on either side of Shelley and me.

Cars lined the roadway, and people made their way up the stone path toward us. Kevin took the basket from my hands. He and Shelley handed roses to each person as they stopped to offer me their condolences. By the end, everyone looked the same, and I wasn't even sure if I was speaking to men or women.

By the time the director got things underway, it seemed half the town was here, but even through the blur, two people were conspicuously missing. I hadn't expected to see Dee after what Shelley had told me, but not seeing Jack hit harder than I expected and added to my sorrow.

My mind wandered through a lifetime of memories, good and bad, as the director spoke. Most of what she said went unheard until my name pulled me back, and I realized we were almost finished. I stepped forward and placed a rose on each of the caskets, then moved back to allow others to do so as well.

Out of the crowd, Jack appeared, tears streaming down his face. He stood for a moment; blue eyes locked with mine. I read the pain they held before he broke his gaze and added his roses to the dozens already thrown. Without another look, he turned, head still down, and strode away. The shredded tissue in my hand no longer contained my tears, and I reached for the only family I had left. Shelley wrapped her arms around me and let me sob.

The tears had all but stopped while the last few people approached to add their roses. As the last one was dropped, an unseasonably cold gust of air whipped across the hilltop and pulled my breath away. The hair on my arms stood on end as the wind caught the heavy flower and pushed it off course just enough for it to miss the shiny wooden box.

At the moment the flower landed, pain slammed into my chest. I stumbled backward as though I'd been shot, my right hand covering my old scar.

Kevin gripped my arm and pulled me into him. "Hey, you okay?"

I nodded. The agony had gone as quick as it had come, and my breath was restored.

I stood in silence, my eyes locked on my parents' graves and my friends around me like a wall of protection. The only marker of time was the gradual departure of the rest of the mourners and the funeral director.

As the four of us left the gravesite, another cold gust blew across the hilltop, and I heard a muffled voice behind me.

"*Eliz abeth … Eliz abeth …*" The wind carried the muffled name to me from someplace distant and unknown.

"Did you say something, Shelley?" I faced my friend.

"No." She shook her head.

"Dave? Kevin?" They, too, shook their heads.

"I could've sworn someone said my name."

\*\*\*

"Shelley, how many people are you expecting?" I said.

A buffet had been set up between the kitchen and living room while we were gone. "There's way too much food here for six of us if Jack and Deanna even show up." I kicked off my shoes and crossed to the sofa to sit down.

"This is just for the inner circle. You're right, it is too much for six, but we'll have leftovers for a couple of days. You can focus on the rest of what needs to be done before you go back to school, and I don't cook, so, whatever." She shrugged and took a few high-ball glasses out of a cupboard in the kitchen. From the shelf below, she grabbed a couple of liquor bottles and added them to the bar. She poured us both a drink, then joined me on the sofa.

"Here, the shot you passed on this morning."

"Thanks." I took the glass from her. "For everything. Not just today either, but all of it, since day one."

"Think nothing of it." Shelley raised her glass in a toast. "Besides, you've been there for me, too, and I know you'd be here if the roles were reversed."

I wasn't entirely sure I would've come back to Evergreen if it were her parents instead of mine. I kept the thought to myself and met her toast before slugging the caramel liquid down in one gulp. I felt the warmth of the bourbon spread as it flowed down my throat and into my entire body while a mild sweetness lingered on my tongue.

The apartment door opened. Dave and Kevin had let themselves in.

"Glasses are on the bar, boys. Help yourselves." Shelley directed them with her drink in hand.

"Did any of you notice if Deanna was at the cemetery? I didn't see her." I set my empty tumbler on the coffee table and sunk into the sofa.

"I didn't see her either." Dave poured a drink for himself and his brother.

Shelley shook her head.

"I thought I saw her, but when I went to find her after, she was gone." Kevin accepted the drink from Dave, and they joined us in the living room.

"I understand she's pissed at me, but she loved my parents. Wouldn't she want to be there for herself, at least, and for you guys?"

"Dee's temper hasn't changed much since high school. You know just as well as the rest of us she doesn't forgive easily and not usually by choice."

38

"You're right, Shelley. I suppose I deserve whatever she feels toward me. It doesn't matter anyway. Not like I plan to see her again after I leave." I helped myself to a refill, then went to the balcony for a smoke.

When I returned to the living room, Jack had joined the group. Prickles ran through my body at the sight of him, and my stomach tied itself in knots. The blood drained from my head, and my heart pounded in my chest, leaving me breathless and light-headed.

"Hi, Jack." I barely recognized my voice over the pounding of my heart. It was thin, as though it were coming through a tin can.

"Liz." His voice was flat, controlled. "I'm sorry about your parents. We're all going to miss them." Jack's body was stiff as he spoke. He made no movement toward me and continued to his conversation with Dave without missing a beat.

The sentiment was so cold and distant; it may as well have come from a complete stranger. I guess that was what we were now—strangers. I hadn't spoken to him in five years, and we hadn't parted on the best of terms.

I sat sideways on the sofa and gazed out the window. In the park across the street, children played as parents and grandparents observed. Silent tears spilled over my eyelids while I watched, knowing I would never share that experience with my own family.

I don't know how long I sat watching the park, but it must have been a while. I was vaguely aware of Shelley talking with the guys, and even less aware of the passage of time.

I jumped at the shrill refrain of Shelley's ringtone. The stark contrast to the voices which had melted into the background startled me out of my daze.

"Come on up. The door's open." I heard Shelley say.

"Dee's on her way up." She put her hand on my shoulder. "You doing okay?"

I realized the light outside had changed and noticed the park was almost empty. I contemplated my glass, still full of a refill which must have been hours old.

"I don't know. What time is it?"

Shelley checked her phone then set it back on the coffee table. "Seven-thirty. Why?"

"I thought I might go lie down, but if I do that now, I'll probably be up all night."

My stomach growled, and I realized I hadn't eaten all day.

"Maybe some food first." Shelley filled a small plate and brought it back for me.

As she handed it over, the door opened. A petite woman with long, fiery red hair entered the apartment and closed the door behind her. She walked over to Dave, Kevin, and Jack. She gave each a long, solid hug then set a bottle with a label I didn't recognize on the counter beside them. Deanna came across the living room toward Shelley and me. The knot in my stomach was instant and massive.

I stood when Shelley did so she could get past me and around the coffee table to greet Deanna with a tight embrace. Before Shelley let go, it appeared as though she turned her head slightly, perhaps to whisper something in Deanna's ear. I thought I saw the slightest nod from Deanna in response before she stepped away from Shelley. Deanna's emerald eyes met mine. Her stare was cold and hard, with no sign of compassion. For a brief moment, she looked as though she might say something, but instead, she closed her eyes for a moment, huffed a loud sigh, then re-joined Jack and the brothers at the bar.

I kept my focus on Shelley. She watched Deanna as she crossed the room and now turned her attention back to me. I stepped toward Shelley and threw my arms around her and held on for dear life. I was afraid if I let go, I might lose her, too.

After a moment, Shelley worked her way free of my grasp. "Liz, it's going to be okay."

"I know. I'm sorry." I rubbed over my scar and wrapped my other arm around my stomach. "I can't do this anymore, Shell, I'm gonna go to bed."

"Of course. You must be exhausted, and I can only imagine how difficult today was for you." She gave me a quick hug then put a hand on my shoulder.

"Thank you again. I love you. You know that, right?"

"I do, and I love you, too, Liz. I'll always be here for you."

I slipped away down the hall, reasonably certain no one else noticed I was gone, and not sure they would even care.

I crawled under the covers and laid my head on the pillow. Even with my eyes closed, the tears seemed determined to flow.

# Chapter 4

I blinked against the harsh reflection of the sun off the snow-covered ground, hugging myself to help protect against the cold. I scanned my surroundings, unsure where I was or how I had gotten here.

*After surveying the area, I realized I was in a clearing surrounded by huge evergreens, fresh snow weighing down their branches. Where I stood, the snow was at least a foot deep. The clearing itself was almost a perfect circle and was quite large, maybe half a mile across. I wondered if it had been man-made.*

*I didn't recall ever being to a clearing like this. I had no idea where I was. I turned around, looking for footprints to follow back to wherever I had started. I squinted against the glare from the sun, which was almost directly above. I cupped my hands over my eyes to shade them and continued my slow turn.*

*When I caught sight of my tracks, I followed them into the tree line. The trees were tall enough to cast shadows, even with the sun almost directly above. I followed my tracks for what seemed like hours when I saw the trees thinning ahead. I increased my pace thinking I must be coming to a road. Instead, a few minutes later, I stepped out of the cover of trees into a circular clearing.*

*"What the hell?" I said aloud.*

*This clearing, like the other, was circular and about half a mile across.*

*"Please tell me this isn't the same clearing. I mean it can't be, can it? How can I start in the clearing and follow my footsteps back to where I started and end up in the same clearing?"*

*My barrage of questions was pointless. There was no one to answer. I was alone out here, and I was lost. I didn't even know if anyone knew I was out here, or if anyone knew where here was.*

*I peered up at the sky, trying to find the angle of the sun so I could estimate the time. To my dismay, it hadn't changed position. How was that possible? I had been trudging through snow for hours, and the sun had been at its peak when I started. I felt like I was losing my mind.*

*I had to get out of here, but how? I searched around and found a stick poking up out of the ground. It cast a small shadow and gave me an idea. I pulled it out of the snow and held it out in front of me, watching the shadow as I hiked. I changed direction, and the shadow moved, too. If I walk straight, the shadow will change position as the sun moves across the sky. It was worth a shot, but first I wanted to make sure I hadn't moved in an arc.*

*I continued, just inside the trees, keeping an eye on the clearing to my right and looking for tracks beside me. Before long, I found a set. I had been walking in an arc! But that also meant I must have started at the clearing. I tracked back again and saw the sun sinking below the trees. I shivered and rubbed my arms against the cold.*

*What the hell is going on? I yelled as loud as I could. The snow muted my voice, and I didn't even get an echo in response.*

*Where was I, and how had I gotten here? The temperature was dropping, and I had nothing to start a fire to keep warm, and no way to find my way through the woods to a road now that it was getting dark. I decided to go with the last resort. If someone was looking for me, they might find me quicker if I stayed put.*

*I found a hollow under a tree and managed to scrounge some branches to cover myself. I sat surrounded by snow and hugged myself tight to preserve my heat as best I could, then shut my eyes and hoped to stay warm enough to survive the night.*

I woke up freezing and blinked my eyes, trying to adjust to the dark. The trees and snow-covered ground around me had disappeared. It was a couple of minutes before I realized I was in the safety and warmth of Shelley's guestroom.

I sat up and drew my knees to my chest. I inhaled deeply, then let it out. Despite the darkness, I saw the white plume of my breath when I exhaled.

*It was just a dream, right?*

Minutes passed while I watched each breath become less visible than the one before. The air in the room warmed as the dream melted away, but the chill in my body didn't abate. I went to the bathroom for some water. I reached for the glass on the counter, and searing pain ripped through my upper chest at the site of my scar. My right hand shot up and covered the area. I massaged the wound for a couple of minutes, and when the sensation subsided, I filled the glass, then gulped the water down between breaths through my nose.

On my way back to bed, I grabbed my journal and a pen from my purse. I climbed into the warmth the bed provided, switched on the bedside lamp, and wrote.

*It's been over five years since the demon's finger sunk into my flesh, and I've never had any pain. Since returning to Evergreen, it's been a different story. Pain has hit me twice now, this time much worse than the first. Maybe it's the stress of being back here, having to bury both my parents, I don't know. The weird thing is my scar looks different, too. It's all red and puffy like it was when it was healing.*

*I've also started dreaming again. Vivid dreams. I haven't had a dream that I remembered since before I left here, but I've had two since coming back. The one tonight was so strange. I was in a clearing in the depth of winter, freezing.*

My eyes tried to pull themselves shut, but I did my best to resist. I wrote a few more words, but my will was losing out. I placed the journal on the nightstand and switched off the light.

\*\*\*

The day after my parents' funeral, I had a meeting scheduled with the lawyer to go over the estate. I had

45

been awake early, and my anxiety caused the butterflies in my stomach to go to war again. I hoped a decent breakfast might help, so I left Shelley's with time to stop at the diner on my way. I picked a small table by the window and sat facing the door to avoid twisting around each time I heard it open. I could see most of the seats in the diner from this spot.

A familiar face in a waitress's uniform marched over.

"Well, well, look what the cat dragged in."

"Deanna. I didn't know you worked here."

"I've been working here since we got outta school, but you wouldn't know that since you didn't bother to keep in touch. What do you want?"

My body prickled all over in response to the tone of her voice, and I was unsure whether she just wanted to take my order or if she meant something else.

"To order." She had taken my delay to respond as confusion. "What do you want to order?"

"Uh, coffee, I guess, and the diner breakfast, eggs over easy with hash browns and sourdough toast." I struggled to get my order out, my brain going a thousand different ways at seeing Deanna.

She scribbled on her pad and stalked away without another word.

I wasn't surprised by the hostility. I hadn't seen Deanna at the funeral, and when she had shown up at Shelley's afterward, she hadn't said a word to me.

I was checking my email on my phone when Deanna brought my coffee a couple of minutes later. She set it down along with a creamer of milk and a bowl of sugar.

46

"Your breakfast will be ready in a couple minutes. You need anything else?"

I eyed the ketchup on the table. "No thanks, I'm good."

A few minutes later, Deanna brought my plate and left me to eat without a word. When she came back with my bill a while later, she sat down across from me.

"How long are you going to be in town?"

"I don't know. I have no idea what I need to do still. Why?"

"I'm not going to pretend I'm happy to see you, so stay out of my way and try not to get anyone killed while you're here." Deanna glanced at the clock on the wall behind me, then shuffled out of the booth and stood up.

"You can pay your bill at the front. I'm on break." She spun on her heel and left.

Deanna had always been a force to be reckoned with. She and her twin sister, Stacey, never hesitated to put someone in their place, whether they deserved it or not. They were most fearsome if you had crossed one or the other because then you had to deal with both of them. The two had shared a real psychic connection which they'd been developing and strengthening, right up to the moment the demon killed Stacey.

I pushed the food around on my plate. Deanna's words and harsh tone had my appetite waning. After a few minutes, I left my unfinished breakfast, paid my bill, and exited the diner with a heavy heart.

\*\*\*

The meeting with the lawyer was straight forward. He didn't expect any contention and felt probate would go through without a problem. My parents had been careful with money, so there was no debt for me to worry about either. In short, my inheritance was enough to get me through the end of school and start my life with a decent nest egg.

As far as the house, property, and contents of both were concerned, they were mine, and I could do with them what I liked. If I wanted to sell, there wouldn't be a problem.

"Might I suggest, though, hang on to the property, at least until you finish school," he said. "I know you don't have long left, but you might need somewhere to live while you are between school and the real world."

"I can't live in Evergreen," I said. "I wouldn't be here now if I didn't have to be. I can't see anything in the next few months changing that."

"You don't need to make any decisions right now," he said. "Do what you need to so you can get closure here, then go back to school, finish your degree, then decide. You have your whole life, and nothing happens to the property until you say so. The last thing you want to do is something you may come to regret down the road."

"Thank you. You've been so helpful with all of this, and I appreciate your advice. I'll think about it." I said. No matter how good the advice was, once I left this time, that was it, I was never coming back.

"I'm always here if you have any questions. Don't hesitate to call."

# EVERGREEN

We shook hands, and I left his small office.

***

I got back to Shelley's with a heavy heart and unsettled stomach. As I entered the apartment, my body tingled. I sat on the couch, not sure if I was about to pass out, cry, or something else altogether.

When the sensation didn't ease within a few minutes, panic took hold. I called the only person I could think of.

"Hey, Liz, what's up?"

"Hey, Shel, do you think you can get the afternoon off?"

"Yea, it shouldn't be a problem. You okay?"

"I'm not sure. I don't want to be alone right now."

"Okay. I'll be home soon."

I hung up and surveyed the apartment. I was surprised when my stomach growled. Hunger had been the furthest thing from my mind with the other symptoms I was experiencing.

I plodded to the kitchen, fearful I might pass out if I moved too fast. The fridge was full of food from yesterday. I picked through and set things on the counter while my mind wandered. Recollections of the past two weeks filtered in. The phone call from the police telling me there had been an accident, my phone call to Shelley. I hadn't been able to speak, but I hadn't needed to, there was only one thing in the world that would take my words away. I tried to remember driving out here, but there was nothing. I had no idea how the traffic had been, what the weather had been like, how long I drove in the dark. Memories of my last two years in Evergreen had taken over most of the drive. All I remembered now was the fog, which, according to the news, was causing burns again.

The hair on my arms stood on end. I closed my eyes and tried to shake my head clear.

A short while later, I was still in the kitchen when I heard footsteps behind me. I gasped and whirled around, a knife in hand.

"Liz, hey, it's me." Shelley stood at the edge of the kitchen, hands raised in defense. She took a step back as she spoke, distancing herself farther from the knife.

My free hand rose to cover my pounding chest. I reached behind me and put the knife on the counter.

"Oh, my God. I am so sorry. You scared the hell out of me."

"Sorry, Liz. I thought you heard me come in." Shelley stepped closer and opened her arms, offering a hug. "Are you okay? I was a bit worried when you called."

I moved in and hugged her, then backed out of it.

"I felt strange after I met with the lawyer, but I'm okay now." I twisted and gestured toward the counter. "I guess I've been pretty deep in thought, but I seem to have put lunch and dinner together for us to take … somewhere."

"Looks good. Where did you have in mind?"

"What about the lake?"

"I haven't been there in a long time." Shelley nodded. "I like it."

We both changed into bikinis, shorts, and a tank top, then gathered towels, a blanket, packed up the food and a few drinks, and headed out.

For the first time in far too long, I was looking forward to what was coming.

We drove out to the lake, singing our favorite songs at the top of our lungs while our hair whipped wildly in the wind. It was perfect, the way it used to be when we first had our licenses, and we didn't have a care in the world.

\*\*\*

We parked in the gravel lot, close to a meadow that led to the lake. A light breeze swept through and filled the air with the scent of wildflowers. Willow branches swept across the grass. At the far end of the meadow, we took the short path through the trees and emerged just a few hundred feet from the lake.

We stopped at the end of the path and surveyed the areas to the left and right. We had most of the lakeshore to ourselves. To the left, there was one, maybe two couples at the far end. To the right, the entire park was empty. We went right, as we always had and picked a spot by the swim dock.

"It's been forever."

"Yeah. I haven't been here since the summer after grad." Shelley put down her bag and pulled out a blanket. She shook it loose, then fanned it over the ground to spread it out.

We ate, neither of us saying much, each with our own memories of this place to unpack.

"I remember the junior barbecue like it was yesterday." Shelley pulled her hair up into a bun.

"That was a great day. It felt like our lives were just beginning. You and Dave were together, Jack and I got together." I started putting containers back in the cooler.

"We finally had freedom. That was the best summer I ever had."

"You said you haven't been out here since senior year. Why?"

"The guys and I came out a couple times with some other kids from school. It was weird without you, Deanna and Stacey, though. I felt like I was cheating. The four of us, Jack, the brothers, and I, came out on our own that August. That was the last time. It almost felt like a memorial. Deanna was in the hospital still, and we practically dragged Jack out of the house. I was getting ready to go away for school, and it felt like the end of things. It felt strange, so I never came back."

"I'm sorry. I didn't know. We didn't have to come here. We could've just gone to the park."

"No, it's okay, Liz. It's good being here with you." She pulled off her shirt, then stood and slipped out her shorts. "Last one in's a rotten egg." She grinned from ear to ear, then took off for the dock before I even had my top off.

I struggled out of my shorts and almost tripped, trying to catch up to her. She dove off the end of the dock before I even reached it. I sprinted down the old wood, and as I neared the end, Shelley came up from her dive. I altered my course and adjusted my steps to jump off the end without stopping. I leaped from the dock, I tucked my knees up to my chest and held tight. I landed in the water a couple of feet from Shelley. A giant splash erupted around me. I dropped into the green depths and let myself sink as far as I could. When my lungs ached for oxygen, I released my knees, pointed my arms skyward, and propelled my body toward air.

I felt the smile on my face and broke the surface with a laugh. I heard the smack of hands on water and turned in time for most of the splash to hit the side of my head.

Shelley and I both laughed as we knocked water back and forth at each other. Sometime later, I pulled my wet hair loose from my face and noticed the wrinkles in my finger. I held them up to Shelley.

"I'm turning into a prune. I think I need to dry off for a while."

Shelley checked her hands and nodded.

"Race you back to the dock." Shelley was already in motion when her words got to my ears.

"You win," I shouted and started a lazy breaststroke toward shore.

"That felt so good." I laid on the dock and draped an arm over my eyes.

"It was amazing." Shelley had beat me back to the dock by at least a minute and was already looking comfortable lying on her stomach.

We laid on the dock and dried in the sun. I marked the passage of time by the gradual warming through my body. The occasional breeze rolled over us from across the lake, then rustled the leaves of trees behind us where birds perched in song.

"Should we invite the guys to come out and meet us for dinner and a fire?" Shelley's voice changed the colors swirling behind my eyelids to a picture of her.

I sat up and opened my eyes to a world washed in reds and greens until they adjusted to the full light of day.

"Sure. It would be nice to see Dave and Kevin again. Tell them to pick up some marshmallows."

# Chapter 5

We'd gotten back to Shelley's before the fog had set in, and neither of us were too tired so we stayed up with a late-night movie and a bottle of wine. It was almost ten the next morning before both Shelley and I were on her balcony with coffee in hand. The air was already hot, and I noticed that the park across the street was quieter than usual.

"Thanks for yesterday, Shelley." I took a tentative sip of my coffee and set it on the small table next to me. "It was just what I needed. It feels like it's been forever since I smiled and meant it."

"It was great. I can't believe Mr. Fire-safety whipped a flaming marshmallow off his stick. Good thing it hit the sand instead of going into the grass," Shelley said.

"I know. Kevin of all people should have known better. The look on his face when he realized it."

"Priceless. So, what's up for today? Do you want to go out to the house?"

"I guess so. The sooner I get it packed up, the sooner I can get it on the market and get out of here."

"I wish you weren't in such a rush. Living in Evergreen isn't that bad, Liz."

"Shelley, it's great that Dave and Kevin have been as supportive as you, but Jack and Deanna both made it pretty clear they want nothing to do with me. That would make for a lot of awkward situations if I moved back here. And let's not forget the reason I left in the first place. What if the demon comes back?"

"We killed it. As for Dee and Jack, I'm sure they would come around if you were here permanently."

"Well, I'm not sticking around to find out. I'm sorry, but I'm not changing my mind."

"All right. Then I guess we better get going. We'll need to stop and get boxes somewhere." She drained her cup and went inside. The stiffness of her stride told me Shelley was hurt, but short of staying in the last place I wanted to be, there wasn't much I could do to change that.

It was a quiet drive, and though I knew it wouldn't last, the tension was palpable. I parked close to the house, and we unloaded the boxes we'd managed to scrounge up on the way.

It wasn't as painful to enter the house today. I was ready for the silence when we stepped through the door. Shelley dropped her boxes on the living room floor, and I did the same.

"Where do you want to start?" Her voice was softer than I expected and provided some relief to the tension from the drive.

"I suppose this is as good a room as any. I don't think it will take too long."

I was right. Despite the size of the room, it was mostly furniture. We had all the knick-knacks and photos packed up in less than an hour.

"Are we taking all this stuff back to my apartment, or do you want to leave it here for now?"

"Might as well leave it here until I figure out what to do with it all."

"Okay, then, what's next?" Shelley ran her fingers through her hair, then pulled it up and tied it back with the elastic she kept on her wrist.

I stood and arched my back, hands on my hips, and considered the rooms beyond the hallway.

"We could tackle the office, but I suspect it will be more of a one-person job. The kitchen is pretty much done, so I guess that leaves the bedrooms, closets, and outbuildings.

"Why don't we pack up your bedroom."

"Yeah, okay."

We each grabbed a couple of more boxes and climbed the stairs to the second floor.

\*\*\*

Shelley stood in front of my bookshelf, well, book-wall. The shelves were partially recessed. My dad had incorporated these bookshelves throughout the house when they built it.

"I'm going to need more than two boxes for all these books and journals," Shelley said. "And a step ladder to get the stuff off the top shelf."

"Yeah, I know. I was raised to read by a writer, though, remember. That comes with a certain

57

expectation that there are going to be a lot of books in one's room."

I left Shelley to the books while I went through my closet and desk.

"I'll have to call someone to pick up all these clothes. I don't think I want anything in here."

"Let me see."

I pulled a couple of tops out and turned to show her. I swapped between them, then tossed them on the bed.

"I agree. Not you anymore. I guess your parents' closet is pretty full, too."

"Probably, but I'm not ready to go in there." I took a deep breath to stifle the nearby tears. "That may end up being a Shelley job."

She nodded and went back to packing my books.

I moved to my desk, and without examining any of it, I packed the small amount left to take back to school with me. I took my last empty box into the upstairs bathroom.

*** 

We arrived back at Shelley's with a couple of boxes from my room. She thought it would be fun to go through my old journals over a bottle of wine, so we set ourselves up on her balcony and dug into our history.

I had been keeping a journal since I was twelve-years old. I don't think I ever missed a day, so there were almost as many of my journals as there were novels. I grabbed the first one out of the box, opened the front cover, and read aloud.

"January 2004. This journal belongs to Elizabeth Porter, Age 12."

This first journal was five years before our trouble had started. The first incident had happened midway through the summer before our senior year, and what followed changed all of us forever.

I flipped the page and read the first entry.

"A new girl started in school today. Her name is Shelley. Mrs. Cooper sat her next to me and asked me to be her buddy this week. I have a feeling Shelley and I will be friends forever."

"That prediction certainly came true. Any others in there?"

I flipped a few pages ahead and read another entry.

"March 5, 2004. Shelley and I have been hanging out a lot. She gets along so well with Stacey and Dee, too. It's like she's always been here like she was supposed to be here all along. Jack and Dave want to hang out this weekend, but I want to have all the girls come for a sleepover. Mom and Dad are going away, and I hate being here by myself. The forest gives me the creeps at night."

"The forest freaked you out even then? I didn't know that."

"We were twelve. I wasn't about to admit to anyone that I had a problem being home alone." I sipped my wine and tipped my chin up at Shelley. "Your turn."

"This one is from 2006. I'll bet it's a much more interesting read." Shelley scanned the pages for an entry to read.

"Here we go. May 28. Shelley has a date with Dave tonight. They're going to the movies. I can hardly wait for all the juicy details. I know she really likes him. Kevin told me Dave's pretty into her, too. I wonder if they'll kiss. Totally unrelated—Dee and Stacey think they are psychic, like actually. They've always had that weird twin thing going on, but Stacey moved something the other day from clear across the room without touching it."

"Wow, boys and psychic powers. Life was safely exciting back then." I lit a cigarette and urged her to keep reading.

"May 29. Shelley's date with Dave went well. She said they sat in the back row of the theater, and they only saw about half the movie! Talk about a marathon make-out session."

"Oh, my God." I laughed so hard I started coughing.

When I regained my composure, Shelley continued.

"Shelley says she really likes Dave. He must be a good kisser because she wasn't so keen on him the other day. And now she wants to set me up with someone so we can double date. We'll see. Maybe I could give Chris from English class a chance. He's pretty cute. Expanding our circle might not be a bad thing."

"Chris was nice," I said, "but he didn't get along with the guys all that well."

"I think that must have had something to do with the fact Jack was jealous of you being with any other guy. You could have dated anyone—it wouldn't have mattered. Jack wouldn't have liked them. And not that it would have happened in a million years, but if you had dated Kevin, I think that would have split the whole group apart."

"Maybe I should have. It might have saved us a whole lot of pain. If we hadn't all been together ..." I let the rest of my thought go unspoken. So much pain had come from the group being together. So many things I wish I didn't remember.

"It may not have made any difference, Liz. If the group had split up, things might have been worse."

"Worse than Stacey dying?"

"We all could have died."

I finished my cigarette in silence as I thumbed through the journal in my hand.

Shelley and I continued reading, and though the laughter returned, fear lurked just beneath the surface, waiting to remind me why I hated this town.

When the color in the sky softened, and a pinkish hue tinted the clouds, we decided to get some dinner. We had spent the entire afternoon reliving our early teens one page at a time, and it had been almost as much fun as Shelley had said it would be.

We continued to peruse the journals after dinner inside the house. The air outside cooled rapidly after the sun went down, and the first hints of the nightly fog were already cropping up.

About ten o'clock, I got up for a bio break. On the way back to the living room, I changed into pj's, and when Shelley saw me, she decided to do the same. I took the opportunity to go out for a smoke. It was dark now, and through the wispy veil, I could see the stars that dotted the sky. In contrast, the park across the street was a void.

I had another cigarette. Goosebumps raised on my arms while I stood at the balcony railing. The moisture in the air kissed my skin. It wouldn't be long before the fog would be too dense to see through.

A breath of air rushed past my ear and made the back of my neck tingle. A shiver had me butt out my smoke before I was ready. I hurried inside and locked the door behind me. I took a last look at the darkness, then grabbed the drapes and pulled them shut.

\*\*\*

The distant ringing of a phone pulled me from a dreamless sleep. I struggled to keep my eyes open while my hand flopped around on the side table for my phone. I checked the screen—no missed calls. It hadn't been my phone ringing. My eyes fell shut, my phone still in hand. There was a knock at the door before I could fall back asleep. The door opened, and Shelley let herself in.

When she didn't say anything right away, I sat up. My friend's face was pale, her expression flat.

"What is it?"

"Dave called." She shook her head as she crossed the room and sat on the end of the bed.

"Kevin asked him to call us. He's busy on a call and wanted us all to know." The evenness of Shelley's tone gave me a bad feeling.

"Know what? Shell, what's going on?" I was fully awake now. My heart fluttered, and nausea crept into my stomach.

"Deanna was trapped in the walk-in freezer at the diner. She's out now, but they're taking her to the hospital in Denver."

The stiffness in her body matched her voice. This was serious.

"They're treating her for hypothermia."

My heart skipped a beat. An image of the frozen meadow from my recent dream flashed in my head. Could it have been about Deanna's incident?

"The thing is, Kevin told Dave Deanna was scared and was saying things that didn't make any sense."

"She doesn't scare easily," I said.

"Yeah, I know. Dave didn't have much more information, but it sounds like Kevin's going to try to stay with her until she's ready to go home." The monotone was gone, and so was some of her stiffness, but there was something in Shelley's demeanor that told me she was worried about more than a possible case of hypothermia. I kept my thoughts to myself as Shelley left my room.

# Chapter 6

Getting back to sleep after Shelley's news wasn't going to happen, so I got out of bed and went to the shower. It was just after nine when I joined Shelley on the balcony.

The cold morning caught me off guard when I stepped outside. My body rippled with one giant shiver, coffee slopped over the edge of my mug, and splatted on the balcony. I rubbed heat into one arm with my free hand as I crossed to the chairs. I set my cup on the table beside Shelley. She'd been smart enough to don a sweater this morning.

"This is kind of a nice change from the heat."

"I guess so. It just reminds me that winter's not far off." Shelley sipped her coffee, a hint of irritation in her voice.

I went back to my room to retrieve a sweater, then detoured through the kitchen for a paper towel to clean up my spill. With that chore complete, I sat next to Shelley to caffeinate.

I watched the activity in the park increase with each sip and let my mind wander unchecked. Memories flowed from one to another. Deanna's face popped in and out, followed by Jack's. Nostalgia crept in and took a firm hold on me. I longed for the days before the demon entered our lives.

My hand jerked when Shelley broke the silence, what remained of my coffee splashed inside my cup.

"What are you going to do today?" Her tone was light, and she sounded much more herself now.

"I should get out to the house and do some more packing, make a list of any repairs that are needed. You?"

"If you don't mind, I'm going to wait here for more information about Dee. See if there's anything she needs when she comes home."

"Yeah, of course. She'll need a friend today. God knows I don't fall on that list anywhere, so you should be here for her. If you do see her, tell her I hope she's okay. I know she may not care, but at least I can put it out there."

\*\*\*

It took me longer than usual to get out to the house. I needed boxes and something for lunch. By the time I was pulling into the driveway, it was close to eleven.

Since Shelley and I had already done my bedroom and the living room, the next point of attack would be the office.

I hadn't been in the office yet. The smell of several leather-bound volumes took me back to my childhood, sitting on my dad's lap in the sizeable reading chair. Several years later, that chair had been replaced by a desk and leather office chair to make dad's writing easier.

I ran my fingers along the spines of several books on the built-in bookcase. It was packed, floor to ceiling with first editions, collector volumes, my dad's complete library of work, and the favorite titles of both he and my mother.

It would be quick work, but it would take several boxes to avoid breaking one's back to move them. The desk and filing cabinet, on the other hand, would take untold hours to sift through.

I sighed at the task ahead and started with the bookcase.

The first shelf I emptied contained several old, leather-bound volumes. My dad had been a collector, and I recalled several of these books being a topic of discussion. They had been expensive to purchase, but Dad had argued they weren't just for him, they were investments. I wrapped each book as though it were a delicate glass ornament and packed them with a heavy heart. Before the bottom of the first box was covered, an errant tear dripped onto one of the covers.

"Shit, shit." I wiped it with the bottom edge of my shirt, terrified it might stain. I managed to set the book on the desk before wet, heaving sobs blinded me.

Images of birthdays and Christmases giving and receiving rare or unique books flashed through my head. Those exchanges would never happen again; my family was gone. I sat on the office floor with my head on my tear-drenched knees, hugged tight to my chest.

When the tears stopped, I cleaned my face and got back to my task. I worked fast to avoid focussing on any one book. If I was ever going to get through this room, I couldn't continue to spend time with my grief after wrapping each tome.

I had just started the last shelf when I heard an engine followed by the crunch of gravel as a vehicle came up the driveway. I left the office and waited on the porch as a truck stopped next to my car.

The engine cut off, and both doors opened. I was delighted to see the Henderson brothers step out in unison. Though they weren't twins, they were often in sync.

I waited on the porch for Dave and Kevin to approach and shook my head as they climbed the steps.

"Shelley told us you were out here by yourself, so we brought refreshments," Dave said as he set a cooler on the porch.

"We also figured you'd be too busy to notice the time and thought we should force you to take a break." Kevin stood tall and stepped in for one of his bear hugs.

"Thanks," I said as he set me down. I took my phone from my back pocket to check the time. "Holy shit, is it really two-thirty?"

"It is." Dave opened the lid to the cooler to reveal about a dozen beer and some snacks. I laughed when I saw the contents.

"I thought you guys said I should be providing the beer."

"You can get it next time," the brothers said together. They eyed one another and grinned.

"Kev, how's Dee? What happened this morning?"

The brothers' grins disappeared.

"She's okay. Shaken up, but by the time we got her to the hospital, her body temperature was back to normal. The doctors released her almost right away."

"I'm glad she's okay."

"Yeah, me too. It always sucks when you have to answer a call for someone you know."

"Did she say what happened?"

"Not at first, but once it was just us, on our way home, she opened up a bit. She said the big oil bucket they use to hold the door got moved. She was pretty freaked about that. She said it weighs something like sixty pounds. She swears there was no way it could have moved by itself. I got the feeling there was more, but her body language was pretty closed off, so I didn't want to push too hard."

"Oh, my God. That's scary. I can't even imagine." I took a sip of my beer to wash down the sandwich.

"Kev, you said Dee's aunt called it in. How did she know?" Dave asked.

"I don't know. I didn't even think about that. I guess we'll have to wait until Dee's ready to talk about it. I haven't seen her this shaken since high school."

Kevin put the last, large bite of his sandwich in his mouth and struggled to start chewing. It made him look like a chipmunk, and I laughed despite the seriousness of the conversation. Kevin often did things without thinking, which had provided us with hours of levity over the years.

Dave snapped a picture with his phone and sent it to Shelley. Kevin raised his brows and tilted his head to one side. With cheeks still full, the expression was comical rather than condemning, and had both Dave and I laughing again.

Appetites sated, we sat on the padded wicker sofa under the living room window, each with a beer in hand, and chatted for a while. Things were never quite as comfortable and relaxed with the few friends I had made in Topeka. I always felt out of place, like something was missing. I wondered if that was something everyone felt with their college friends.

"So, how's it going in there?" Dave asked before taking a long pull off his beer.

"Pretty good, I think. Shelley and I packed the living room and my bedroom yesterday, and the office bookshelf is almost empty."

"Anything we can do to help?" Kevin asked as he finished his beer.

"I don't know. Most of what's left is going to involve a lot of decision making. There's so much to do out here, too. I don't even know where to start."

"Well, if you're seriously planning on selling the place, you're going to need an inspection. Dave and I can do that for you while we're here if you want."

"How can you guys do a building inspection?"

"We just got certified and registered with the state. Figured it was a good addition to what we already do."

"That would be great then. I'm sure you'll find something that needs repair, the place isn't new anymore. While you're looking around, if you see anything you want, tools or whatnot, let me know. I'm sure I won't have use for a lot of this stuff."

After a few more minutes sitting on the porch, Kevin got up and went to the truck. He returned with a metal case roughly the size of a sheet of paper but about two inches thick. He opened the lid and pulled out a pen and a paper, which he clipped on to the cover. He seemed quite serious about the inspection.

The brothers decided to start with the outbuildings. While they headed out to the yard, I finished my beer and had a smoke before returning to the books.

When I knelt to finish the bottom shelf, I noticed the last few books weren't sitting right up against the back. I removed a few of them and saw something tucked in behind. I grabbed it and recognized it as soon as it came in full sight. Ice filled my veins, and the hair on the back of my neck stood on end. I stared at the journal in my hand and tried to reconcile the impossibility.

*How the hell did this get here? Did I imagine it at Shelley's? I know I was tired and spooked by the fog. Maybe my imagination conjured it. I had just woken from a nightmare about that day.*

As I tried to rationalize what I thought I had seen that first night in town, a tickle hit the middle of my spine.

I spun around, looking for whoever was watching me, but found the room empty. I stood, threw the journal into an open box, and rushed from the room. I hurried through the living room and out the door. As soon as I was on the porch, I struggled to light a cigarette with trembling hands. I paced back and forth for a few minutes, then decided I didn't want to be alone.

I rushed toward the old barn, trying not to run, my spine still tingling. I found Dave and Kevin inside.

"How does it look, Dave?" I asked, trying to sound calm.

"It's in good shape. Better than I thought it would be. Your parents did a great job of maintaining this barn, and the roof is almost brand new."

"I think they replaced it last summer. Dad said they were replacing all the roofs, one per year. He did most of the work himself to save some money."

"Well, he did a great job with this one," Dave said. "You'd never know he wasn't a professional."

I wandered with them as they finished up and made their way through the shed and then to the garage. It took over an hour, but whenever I looked at the house, I still got spooked.

Dave and Kevin were ready to look through the house before I was. I convinced them to take another beer break. After half an hour of stalling, I hesitated, then followed them into the house.

The brothers split up. I toured through the house with Kevin and watched as he took notes and made lists of repairs and cosmetic updates, which would help my sales value.

By the time we met back up with Dave, several hours had passed since I'd found the journal. Still, I had no desire to be here alone and decided to follow them back to town.

\*\*\*

When I entered Shelley's apartment, Deanna was on the couch with Shelley. My stomach flipped. Deanna's wrath had always been something to fear. I had never been on the receiving end before, but it wasn't something to take lightly.

When the door shut, Deanna's gaze shifted to me. Even from this distance, I saw fire in her eyes. She didn't acknowledge me. Instead, she turned back to Shelley.

"I'm going to be at my aunts' for a few days," Deanna said. "They've insisted. Maria said they have some things they want to discuss. I'll call you later." Deanna and Shelley exchanged hugs, then Deanna stood and stormed passed me on her way out.

I took her place next to Shelley.

"Her opinion of me hasn't eased. So much for coming around." I made air quotes around the last two words.

"I said eventually, *if* you were here permanently, remember?" Shelley's voice was soft, almost apologetic.

"How is she?"

"Pretty shaken and scared, but physically, she's fine."

"Did you get any details from her? Kevin said she didn't say much."

"She said," Shelley took a breath and paused as though trying to decide what to say. "She said she felt a presence in the diner when she got there. She smudged it and thought she'd cleansed the place. Clearly, that wasn't the case."

"What, you mean, the smudge didn't work? How does she know?"

"She swears up and down there is no way that bucket could've moved on its own, and there was no one else in the building."

"Okay, so if there was a spirit in there with her, why would it lock her in the freezer?"

"Don't know, but that's why she's scared." Shelley shrugged, then shook her head. "It would've had to be extremely powerful or vengeful to escape the smudge and move that bucket."

"Kevin told me Dee's aunt called in the report. Why didn't Dee just call?" I said.

"She didn't have any cell service. She said all she could think was that she was going to die in that freezer. Then she started thinking about her aunts and how upset they'd be to lose both the girls. Next thing she knew, Kevin was banging on the door."

"Really? Do you think her ESP is coming back?" I said.

"What other explanation could there be?"

I shivered.

Shelley stood and picked up the two empty cups off the coffee table.

"I'm feeling the need for something a bit stronger than tea. Join me in a glass of wine?"

"You really need to ask?" I shifted on the couch and got more comfortable.

"How did it go at the house today?" she asked from the kitchen.

"Fine, I guess. I got most of the books in the office packed, and Dave and Kevin came by for a while."

"That's nice. Did they help you pack?"

Stephanie Galay

"No, but they did a full inspection of all the buildings and gave me a list of repairs. Kevin said he'd even order the materials and supplies for me."

"That's great." Shelley handed me a glass and sat down next to me.

"It was nice to have some company out there." I swirled the wine and watched the deep red legs linger on the sides of the glass, then took a long sip. "I found something that unnerved me—a journal. I thought I had seen it here in the spare room the night I got here. It was one of the ones we used senior year."

"Are you sure that's what it was? I thought we burned all that stuff after Stacey's funeral."

"I didn't read any of it, but it seems we missed one. There was no mistaking it. It was stuck behind a bunch of books in my dad's office."

"If you saw it here, how did it get to your house?"

I shook my head and hunched my shoulders.

We both sat in silence, just looking at one another.

"Are you hungry?" My stomach growled, almost on command. "Cause I could use something to eat."

"I could eat."

"I know there's still food in the fridge, but I'm craving Dim-Sum." I said.

"Sounds good to me. Sam's is still the best around."

"Isn't Sam's still the only one around?"

"Yeah, but my way sounded better."

# Chapter 7

When I parked my car at the house on Monday morning, the uneasiness I'd had the day before was forgotten. Caffeine coursed through me, and my steps across the yard were light and full of energy.

Inside, I plugged my phone into the stereo and turned up the volume. The music made the work much more pleasant.

After a couple of hours, I had a stack of paperwork on the desk to ask the lawyer about, and the filing cabinet was almost empty. As I danced my way to the kitchen for a glass of water, the doorbell rang.

I retraced my steps and opened the door to the bluest eyes I've ever seen. My stomach dropped, and my extremities tingled.

"Jack. What are you doing here?" My heart raced.

"Delivery. The supplies Kevin ordered for you. I thought I would bring them out myself."

"Uh, thank you." I stood dumbfounded, holding on to the door with my right hand.

"Can I come in and put this box somewhere? It's getting heavy." He shifted his weight, then rearranged his grip, and lifted a knee to support the bottom of the box.

"Oh, yes, of course. Sorry." I pulled the door wider and stepped out of the way to let him through. "Just put it anywhere, I guess. Sorry, I wasn't expecting this stuff so soon. I imagined Kevin would bring it all when he and Dave came to do the work."

Jack set the box down in an empty corner of the living room, then faced me. A mix of excitement and anxiety washed over me when our eyes met.

"He was going to, but I thought we should talk, so I'm here instead."

Butterflies erupted in my stomach.

*What could he possibly want to talk about after all this time when he passed up two opportunities already?*

"I'll go get the rest of the order." Jack moved toward the door.

"Do you need a hand?"

"No, it's fine." Jack's voice still sounded distant and emotionless. I was sure no one else in the world would have noticed. He was out the door before I could argue, clearly wanting to get the business part of this visit out of the way.

I left the door open, stopped the music, and went to get some water for both of us. It took Jack three more trips to bring in all the boxes. When he finished, I gestured toward the porch. I wasn't sure I wanted to sit in the living room for this conversation. There was already too much emotion in that room.

Jack sat on the sofa under the window, and I handed him one of the glasses. I opted to sit next to him, so I wouldn't have to look him in the eye. As soon as I sat down, the hair on my arm prickled. The spark was still there, and I couldn't help but wonder if he felt it, too.

"You said you wanted to talk. Why didn't you just talk to me after the funeral?"

"It wasn't the time or place for this conversation."

A lump rose in my throat.

*Be strong, Liz. No matter how bad this gets, don't let him see your pain.*

"I'm listening."

I heard him pull in a deep breath and, from the corner of my eye, saw him run his fingers through his chocolate hair. He bent his head, and I knew he was looking for the strength to get through a speech he had probably practiced for hours. I clicked my thumbnails against each other, bracing myself.

"I didn't think I would ever get the chance to say this, but you're a bitch."

"What?" A personal attack was the last thing I expected, and it sent pins and needles through me.

"You are a bitch. The way you left, the non-discussion, the one-sided end to our relationship. You may not have ended my life, but you killed me that day. I am angry, hurt, resentful. I've been through hell and had to claw my way back to functional. Seeing you at the funeral twisted everything up inside and brought all the anguish back. You're a bitch."

I felt the familiar sting of tears in my eyes. I clenched my teeth and crossed my arms because these tears were different. There was anger and defensiveness in these tears. I had no idea how to respond, so I didn't. When the silence became my voice, Jack continued.

"I never understood why I didn't get a say in trying to stay together. Dee and I commiserated about it for months. Why you wouldn't maintain contact with us, but you did with Shelley. At first, I was just hurt, devastated, then I got angry." When I lifted my gaze, he had twisted toward me. His blue eyes were steel gray, and his stare drifted across the space between us. This time it was moths in my gut, and the look in his eyes transformed them to nausea.

"After about a year, I just didn't care anymore. My heart had been ripped out, no chance of ever loving anyone else because there was just no feeling anything. Then you showed up, and it all came rushing back."

"Jack, I'm sorry." As soon as I unclenched my jaw to speak, the tears spilled free. I let them flow, resisting the urge to acknowledge them. "I needed to detach from the people that might bring me back. I was terrified, if I stayed here or allowed myself to come back, the demon might, too. I couldn't take that chance and never imagined having to come back, ever."

"Yeah, you said that when you left, but it doesn't make anything any better. You made decisions for all of us, without thought of how any of us might feel. You were selfish and keeping in touch with Shelley just made it worse."

"Shelley is like a sister to me. Would you ask Dave or Kevin to give up contact with the other?"

"Deanna had to. Stacey died. Her real sister, her twin, her actual other half. Shelley might be an excellent friend, but that's all she is. She's not your sister."

# EVERGREEN

His words slapped me in the face and tore into my soul. I buried my face in my hands, with my head hung low. I couldn't speak for the shards of glass in my throat, and I couldn't look at him. He didn't say anything else. I'm not sure how long we sat next to each other in silence, but I stayed buried in my hands until I heard him get up, walk across the gravel to his car, and drive away.

*\*\**

When the tears dried up, I locked the house. There was no point in even pretending I was okay enough to work any longer. I got into my car and lit a cigarette. I tried desperately to rid Jack and his tirade from my mind as I drove back to Shelley's, but it was impossible. I couldn't look forward without seeing his eyes in the sky ahead of me. Those amazing blue eyes just kept staring at me, full of pain and anger, the whole way back to town.

Shelley was at work, so I let myself into her apartment. I grabbed a glass, and the first bottle I laid my hands on, and went out to the balcony. I sat and poured myself a drink. Focused on the park across the street, I threw the whole thing down my throat and started over. The refill lasted about three mouthfuls, each consecutive refill lasting longer. I was just finishing my fourth or fifth shot when Shelley got home from work. The ashtray beside me was almost full, and the bottle, though not full to start, was just about empty.

"Bad day?"

I sipped, emptied the bottle into my glass, and raised it above my head. "I'll replace it."

"What happened?"

"Jack happened."

"Jack? What do you mean?"

I pointed at her with my glass. "Don't tell me you didn't already know I was the world's most selfish bitch." I nodded, emptied the glass, and set it down a little too hard. "Him and Deanna bonded over it, you know."

Shelley sat on the seat next to me, and I slurred my way through the horrid encounter. My chest tightened as I spoke, anger and sadness at war.

"Just anger, no forgiveness or anything else? I had no idea he was that upset, Liz. Every time we talked, he'd ask how you were, what you were up to. Honestly, I always got the feeling he was still in love with you."

"Guess not. Not that it would matter." I stood then stumbled toward the railing. I somehow managed to grab on and hold myself up.

"Where are you going?" Shelley was on her feet and halfway to me with her arms out.

"Bottle's empty. Need another drink."

"Yeah, I don't think so. Come on. I'm putting you to bed. You can have a nap, and I'll get us some dinner." She wrapped one arm around my waist and pulled my arm around her neck.

"Fine." Not that I was getting much choice at this point.

Shelley guided me while I staggered through the apartment to my room. She helped me to the side of the bed, then let me flop face-first onto it.

Oblivion engulfed me.

\*\*\*

I woke with a jolt, my shoulder on fire with pain. The remnants of another nightmare of the battle we'd had with the demon lingered, and I struggled to get my bearings in the dark room.

My head pounded so hard I could almost hear the thumps. I reached a hand up to my temple, the image of the demon's face was replaced by that of an empty liquor bottle followed by Jack's face.

*Oh, right. The Jack attack.*

The throbbing in my shoulder interrupted and forced me from my bed. As I trudged to the bathroom, I pulled my shirt off and swore under my breath when the muscles surrounding my wound resisted the movement.

A large area around my scar was deep red. I leaned forward for a better look in the mirror and noticed tiny, faint circles above and below the scar line, which resembled the marks left by stitches.

*It looks like it's un-healing, but that's impossible.*

I rubbed my eyes and inspected it again. I wasn't hallucinating; the stitch marks were there. Streaks of pain shot inward when I pressed around the edges of the wound. I backed away from the counter and worked my shoulder in circles, then my arm. Each rotation pulled at the muscles in my chest, adding to the pain instead of easing it.

I swallowed a couple of Ibuprofen with a long drink of water, then switched off the light and went back to bed. With any luck, the pills and more sleep would make me feel better.

# Chapter 8

I t was after nine when I padded down the hall to the kitchen. A note from Shelley lay on the counter next to the coffee maker.

*Sorry Liz - had to go in to work this morning. I'll call you later. Have a good day.*

The note was a great find. I hadn't wanted to talk to Shelley about my scar or the dreams. Having a day to think about it was a good thing.

***

I sat on my porch, taking a break from the paperwork in my dad's office when a car pulled into the driveway. I wasn't expecting anyone, so I put my cigarette out and moved to the steps.

I reached the bottom step as the car came to a stop next to mine. I couldn't tell who occupied the vehicle until she stepped out.

"Deanna?" I strode out to meet her halfway, unsure of her intentions after our previous meeting.

She marched across the gravel toward me, determination written all over her small frame.

"Don't take this the wrong way," I started, "but what are you doing here? I thought you didn't want to have anything to do with me?"

"This visit wasn't my idea. After what happened at the diner, my aunts said I should at least explain myself. They said I owed you that much."

"Owed me? Why?"

"Something happened the other day when I was locked in the freezer at work." She paused, and I nodded.

"The only reason I made it out of there is I somehow managed to communicate with one of my aunts, telepathically. I haven't been able to do that since ..." She tilted her face skyward.

"Dee," When I spoke, she brought her gaze back to mine, lifted her hand, and cut me off before I could even get her name out. I shut my mouth and let her continue.

"My telepathy went away after that battle. You knew that, I think. The last little while, I've been getting hints of people's emotions, but nothing like I used to. I don't know how or why, but I think it might all be coming back."

"Deanna, I don't understand. Why are you telling me this?"

"After the whole freezer incident, my aunts said I should forgive you, or at least come and talk to you. I'm not saying we are back to being best friends, but I don't hate you. I have been angry at you for a long time, though. Some difficult conversations and introspection have persuaded me to concede, my anger has been misdirected. I know Stacey wasn't your fault, but I blamed you. I know it could just have easily been Shelley or Jack or any of us." Deanna glared at her clenched fist.

When she focussed on me again, she must have read the confusion in my expression.

"When I heard about your parents, it all came rushing back to me. Emotions I had worked hard to overcome. I knew you'd be back, but when I saw you at Shelley's after the funeral ..." She stared at the ground for a moment, then back at me. "There was so much rage because you hadn't come back for a single holiday, or even the first anniversary of Stacey's ..."

I could hear the pain building as her voice caught on her sister's name. Deanna paused, then took a deep breath. I figured she was stuffing her grief back down where she could manage it. I've had lots of practice at that in recent days.

"You didn't come home for the anniversary of Stacey's death or anything else. It was like none of us meant anything to you, or at least not enough for you to acknowledge we still existed. You never even came home to see your parents, but there you were, sitting in Shelley's living room. I'm not sure if I expected you to stay here, or in a hotel, but I didn't expect to see you there."

I didn't respond. There was nothing to say. Silence and tension filled the space between us. I glanced around, needing to break eye contact, then gestured toward the house. We crossed the short distance in silence and sat on the porch sofa.

"How could you just stay away like that, Liz? I really needed you, and you were just gone."

I picked at a broken edge on the armrest. "I needed to heal after what we went through, and Washburn was my way out."

"Washburn was an excuse. Why didn't you at least keep in contact? You kept talking to Shelley."

"I needed to forget. I almost died, too, remember? Leaving you guys was agonizing, but I had to, I didn't want any reminders. Why do you think I broke up with Jack? Shelley had a life outside Evergreen for a long time, so keeping in touch with her somehow made sense and kept me sane. I mean for Christ's sake, Dee, we were eighteen, and we fought a demon the rest of the town didn't even know existed. I barely survived. Why would I *not* want to forget that?"

"But you did survive. And that whole wanting to forget my *sister* died, my *twin*. She was part of me. You *know* how hard that was for me, you saw what I went through, or did you forget that my aunts had me hospitalized?"

"Dee, I didn't mean I was the only one. I haven't forgotten any of it despite my efforts, believe me. You don't know the things I've done to try to forget."

"So how could you abandon us, your friends?"

"I didn't see it as abandoning you," I said. "I was trying to escape a time in my life that I couldn't bear having memory of. Seeing you in so much pain every day and living with the secret we were keeping from our families and the rest of the town—I don't know if I really planned to be gone forever, but once I got to Topeka and got into a routine, it got easier and easier to pretend it had all been a bad dream, so I stayed away."

"But you still kept in touch with Shelley."

"She's always been *my* other half. You know that. She may not be blood, but she's my sister, and she is my therapy when I can't ... when I *couldn't* talk to my parents."

"Well, you were my therapy, so you can imagine how things got for me. I guess that's why I've spent the better part of the last five years harboring an epic grudge against you."

I thought for a moment that I saw a tear betraying her, but Deanna ran both hands up her face, beginning at either side of her nose and ending with brushing her long red hair back over her forehead.

"I'm not going to apologize for leaving, but I am sorry you felt abandoned. I never meant to hurt you or anyone else. To be honest, I wasn't thinking about what impact it would have on the rest of you. I just had to get away."

Deanna lowered her gaze and rubbed her hands together. The conversation hadn't been easy for either of us. I could tell she was contemplating what I had said.

"I guess I can imagine how leaving was the best medicine for you, but I have scars that are your fault, and I'm not sure how to fix that between us."

"So, where do we go from here?"

"I guess a lot of that depends on you and how long you're in town. I'll play nice, but don't expect me to trust you. If you want that back, you're going to have to make me believe you deserve it."

"I suppose that's fair. Dee, I am sorry that my leaving made things so much worse for you."

"I'm sorry about your parents, Liz. It was painful to lose Stacey, but I can't imagine how it would feel to lose both your parents at once. I don't know what I'd do if I lost any of my aunts, never mind all of them at once."

She stood and strolled to her car without saying goodbye. I watched her drive away, her words echoing in my mind.

# Chapter 9

Once Deanna was out of sight, I went to the large vegetable garden to do some weeding. I thought about what she had said as I ripped weeds from the soil and recalled the few days before I left Evergreen.

My mind's eye showed me people's reactions as I said my goodbyes. I hadn't noticed at the time, but reflecting, I could read the pain on most of the faces. Though some accepted my decision, I realized now, that most, including my parents, likely hadn't agreed with it. I would do what I could to reconcile with Deanna and Jack, but I'd lost the opportunity with my mom and dad.

The unpleasant trip down memory lane wasn't doing me any favors. The hair on the back of my neck stood on end. The tingle worked its way over every part of my body.

I glanced around. Was there someone just beyond the trees? I left the garden, almost at a run, and continued to scan the yard as I hurried up the porch steps. I did a full circuit around the house, paying particular attention to the tree line at the back of the property.

Satisfied I was alone, I sat on the sofa under the living room window and lit a smoke. I took a deep calming drag, then heard my stomach growl, a reminder I hadn't eaten yet.

I was able to put my thoughts aside long enough to find something to eat. Twenty minutes later, with my hunger satisfied, my mind started picking at the thread of fear.

The thread pulled at memories which had been safely stored away for the past five years, plucking at the layers which I had worked hard to build. Burying those memories had been necessary to protect myself, so I could live a normal life away from here, away from my family and friends, where I tried to be happy. The past ten days had already pulled the thread loose, but sitting here, dwelling on the past, it was unraveling faster than a shooting star.

The softness of the cushion beneath me and the penetrating afternoon heat soon took effect. My eyes and limbs felt heavy. I felt myself slip in and out of consciousness. Then blackness took over.

***

*We were in homeroom when the sirens started. An announcement came over the PA system that we were being sent home. Something about several teachers needed elsewhere. The classroom erupted; everyone spoke at once.*

*"... that many sirens ..."*

*"How many teachers?"*

*"... go see what's going on."*

*The halls emptied, and my friends and I decided to find out what was happening. We exited the building and saw thick, black smoke above the trees. We took off toward what must be a massive fire. The closer we got, the more people we encountered, and the faster the growing crowd moved.*

*Acrid wisps of smoke filled the air. It caught in my throat, and I started to cough. Jack handed me a bottle of water. I let the liquid run down my throat and ease the assault.*

*We were close to the source of the billowing smoke. A general panic spread through the crowd and grew with each passing block. Cell phones rang and buzzed while dozens of conversations added to the chaos. The wave of people moved as one until we reached the fire, and the mass spread out in front of the four-story apartment building.*

*It seemed as though all the fire trucks and police cars in town were at the scene. Uniforms scrambled in every direction. People pressed toward several officers who were trying to set up a barricade. Unanswered questions were shouted over one another.*

*Three cars pulled up, and several of our teachers jumped out, helmets in hand, already in their gear. They rushed to the command truck to sign in.*

*The large group watched helplessly, many in tears, as the fire crew worked feverishly to get control of the blaze. The roar of the fire grew as flames dipped and jumped, orange and red tendrils reaching for new fuel.*

*A deep rumble joined the crackling of flames. The sound grew louder and moved through the building. Shouts and commands from several crew members erupted into the air. Firefighters clung to ladders as they were retracted and pulled away from the fire. Seconds later, a section of the roof collapsed into the building and sent a tower of sparks and thick, dark smoke into the sky. Screams from the crowd filled our ears.*

*"We should go, I don't think it's safe to be standing around watching this." I grabbed Jack's arm and backed away.*

*"Liz is right," Jack said. "We should get outta here."*

*My friends and I ran until we could no longer hear the crowd. When we reached the park in the center of town, we agreed to share any information we came across, then went our separate ways.*

*Shelley, Jack, and I wandered back to her place. Jack held me tight and stroked my hair until I was no longer shaking. He loosened his arms and leaned back just far enough to kiss me. His lips were soft and warm against mine. All my worries melted away.*

*The three of us said goodbye. Shelley and I watched as Jack turned and stepped off the sidewalk. A dark red shadow appeared in front of him. I tried to yell out a warning, but I was too late. I watched in horror as the shadow swallowed Jack in its depths.*

*All I could do was scream.*

\*\*\*

My body jerked. I opened my eyes and peeked around, confused. I was sitting on the porch sofa but expected to be in front of Shelley's childhood home.

*Not again. These dreams have got to stop.*

My neck ached. I tilted my head from side to side in an attempt to relieve the kinked muscles.

The dream lingered, and a sour knot formed in my stomach. I stood and covered my mouth with a hand, not sure if my nausea would rise or not. I waited for a moment, then ran for the bathroom.

When my body stopped heaving, I rinsed my face with cold water and brushed my teeth. I tapped my toothbrush on the sink and straightened in front of the mirror. The stitch marks above and below my scar, were barely visible this morning. Now they were prominent, and the color around the rest of the site was a deep red.

I went to the kitchen and filled a glass from the tap. My gaze focused on the treeline at the back of the property. The trees were still locked together as if to guard a secret. Just beyond was the meadow where we'd fought the demon. The feeling of unease I had woken with persisted.

I needed to get out of here.

# Chapter 10

A few minutes from Shelley's building, a fire truck raced toward me, lights flashing. As it passed, its sirens drowned out the music from my stereo. I started to roll up my window, but by the time my finger found the button, the sirens were already a distant wail.

My palms were slippery on the steering wheel, and my heart raced. I pulled over and changed direction to follow the fire truck. I had to know where it was going. I smelled the pungent air before I saw it. I drove toward the column of dirty, black smoke, and choked on the occasional breath. It didn't take long to realize the truck was going to the same building from my dream.

When I got within a block, I parked my car and walked the rest of the way. A barricade was up, and dozens of people stood on both sides. Those on the inside were residents. Faces buried in hands, people embraced, devastated, and tried to console one another. Through muffled voices around me, I heard the suspicions of onlookers and people looking for loved ones on the other side of the barrier. There hadn't been a fire this bad in several years.

Out of the crowd, I heard my name. I stretched to tiptoes and scanned the area. Shelley ran toward me.

"That's Jack's building." Her words floated past me, mostly unheard.

"Shelley, that's the same building as before." I gawked at her. She must have read the terror in my eyes.

"I'm sure it's just a coincidence." I knew she was trying to reassure me, but I heard the doubt in her voice.

When we approached the barricade, I stopped short and yanked on Shelley's arm. The force spun her around to face me.

"Wait." Her previous piece of information sunk in. "What do you mean, this is Jack's building?" I scanned the crowd of people on both sides of the barricade. "Shelley, practically the whole building is engulfed, and I don't see Jack! Tell me you meant he owns this building." I knew he didn't.

All she could do was shake her head. My heart skipped a beat, my stomach dropped, and I thought I was going to be sick. Shelley pulled her phone from her back pocket and dialed.

"Come on, pick up, pick up." A few more seconds and she shook her head. "He's not answering."

We moved closer to the fire crew, hoping to catch someone to speak to, or find Kevin. When I didn't see him or his name on any of the uniforms, I tried calling him, but as I expected, he didn't answer.

*He must be part of the crew on the ladders or the roof.*

Shelley called Jack's cell again while I kept struggling to get someone's attention, but he still didn't answer.

It took a while, but we managed to flag down a sheriff's deputy.

"A friend of ours lives in this building and is unaccounted for," Shelley said with surprising calm.

"What floor does your friend live on? I'll go see what I can find out for you."

"He lives on four," Shelley said. "His name's Jack Mitchell."

The deputy scribbled in his notebook and hurried off.

Neither of us spoke, afraid to voice thoughts we didn't want to think, and waited for the deputy to come back with something, anything. All around us, residents and loved ones cried, friends and neighbors tried to console one another, spectators and volunteer crews still ran up to the scene. I scanned the crowds again, hoping to have missed Jack with all the confusion.

Shelley dialed his number, but still got no answer. After what seemed an eternity, and more unanswered attempts to call Jack, the deputy returned, stoic.

"I'm sorry, miss, the fire crews can't enter the building right now. The fire's too hot. With this intensity, it will be a few days before investigators will be able to go in. They'll need to make sure the building is stable and safe for crews."

My head spun, vision blurred, and my knees buckled. I don't know whether Shelley held me up or if the deputy did. The next thing I knew, I was sitting on the sidewalk with my head between my knees.

When my sight focussed, the first person I saw was Deanna. When my mind cleared, I saw Dave and Shelley a few feet away. Dave stood close to her, his hand resting on her shoulder, his head bent as though consoling her. I could tell they were speaking, but I couldn't hear what they said.

"Deanna?"

She didn't respond, just stared at me, her eyebrows furrowed. After a few more seconds, her eyes lit up, and one corner of her mouth curved upward. She seemed amused.

"What? What do you know?"

"You have feelings for him." It wasn't a question. "You were terrified when I got here. I could feel it from a mile away." Her expression smoothed, but one side of her mouth remained curled.

"So, what if I have feelings for him? Can't I be concerned about his well-being?" I heard the defensiveness in my voice and folded my arms across my chest.

"It wasn't *concern* that I felt, Liz. It was anguish, like the type a person feels when they've lost a loved one."

There was nothing I could say, denial was useless. I watched Shelley and Dave for a moment, then turned my attention back to Deanna.

"Any word from him yet?" I asked.

"No, not yet. Shelley keeps trying, but …" She offered me a hand. I took it, and she pulled me off the ground. "I'm sorry, Liz. It's not looking good." Worry replaced the amused look she'd worn.

The four of us staked the scene for what seemed like hours. One of us tried Jack's cell every twenty minutes or so. It was late afternoon when we resolved to try Jack one last time before retreating to Shelley's apartment. We all knew what it probably meant if he didn't answer.

"Jack! Oh, thank God. Where the *hell* are you?" Shelley waved at us to gather around her. We all perked up and listened, collectively exhaling. "Are you okay?" she paused. "Because we're all sitting outside your apartment watching it burn. Your building's on fire, Jack." Another pause. "Yes, seriously. I've been trying to get a hold of you for hours. We were all starting to think you might be dead. Didn't you get a call from the sheriff's office or anything?" Shelley stared at me, then Deanna. "Well, I'm sorry to be the one to give you the bad news, but from where I'm standing, the damage looks like it's going to be extensive."

As Shelley continued on the phone with Jack, Dave pulled Deanna and me into a three-way hug. Relief coursed through me and chased away the prickles of dread which had surfaced when I'd realized Jack was missing.

Shelley put her phone in her back pocket, and threw her hands up, both in relief and frustration, as she joined the group.

"Jack's safe. He's been in Denver with his brother all afternoon. He didn't even know about the fire until right now."

"I'll get what information I can from Kevin tonight," Dave said. "Though, it may not be much."

Our small group dispersed. Shelley and I drove back to her apartment in silence. I was unwilling to voice my concern about what this fire could mean, and the fact Shelley wasn't talking led me to believe she might have a similar thought.

\*\*\*

A little before seven, Shelley decided it was time to get something to eat. We agreed on pizza, and she opted to go pick it up. I took the opportunity to have a shower. The two glasses of wine I'd had in the short time since we'd left the fire hadn't calmed my nerves. A hot shower always seemed to wash away my stress, fear, and anxiety, even if only for a few hours.

I stood under the flow, my eyes closed tight, and breathed deep to clear my mind. It didn't take long for the water to work its magic. I swept the liquid off my face and over the top of my head. I let it take my stress down the drain with it. I didn't know how long the relief would last, but at the moment, I didn't care.

When I had dried off, I noticed the heat of the day had eased, so I got dressed in a pair of sweats and a light hoodie. I threw my towel-dried hair into a messy bun and made my way out to the kitchen to pour myself another glass of wine.

Stephanie Galay

The sliding door was open, so I took the almost empty bottle with me as I went to join Shelley on the balcony.

"Do you want another glass of wine?" I watched my feet navigate over the track. Once I stepped over the threshold, I looked forward and saw a man, not Shelley, at the railing facing toward the park across the street.

The man turned to me. I almost dropped both the bottle and my full glass as my heart jumped into my throat.

"Jack? What are you doing here? Shelley said you were in Denver with your brother."

"I was, but after she called me about the fire, I decided I needed to be here." His voice tied my stomach in knots.

"Is Shelley back, how did you get in?"

"I have a key. When Shelley didn't answer the buzzer, I let myself in. Where did she go?"

"Uh, to pick up dinner." My mind reeled. My entire body tingled, and I felt weightless, almost dizzy.

*What the hell is he doing here?* I thought.

Jack shifted awkwardly, taking a couple of steps toward me. "Shelley offered me a room." It was as though he'd read my mind. "I told her I could stay with one of the guys, but she wouldn't have it."

I lifted the bottle of wine to my lips and took a long drink, trying to think of something to say.

"If it bothers you, I can go stay with one of the brothers, I'm sure they won't mind," Jack said.

I regarded the bottle and realized what I had done. "No. No, it's fine." I gestured with the bottle. "Wrong

100

EVERGREEN

hand." A small, nervous laugh escaped my throat. "I was just surprised to see you here, that's all. Shelley didn't tell me she offered you a room. You did know I was staying here, right?"

The apartment door slammed shut before Jack could answer. I spun around to see Shelley coming down the hall, her hands full with a large pizza box and a heavy-looking bag. She lifted them a few inches when I started toward her.

"Dinner is served, my dear. Extreme veggie lovers on thin crust, just the way you like it."

I glanced at Jack, then spun and hurried inside. I crossed the room and met Shelley in the kitchen.

"Why didn't you tell me you offered him a room?" I spoke in a whisper in case Jack had followed me in. "I would have gone back to the house when you left if I'd known he was coming." That little glint appeared in Shelley's eyes again.

"I know you would have." She grabbed plates from the cupboard and set them on the bar. "We've been drinking, so I didn't want you to drive. Besides, I didn't realize he was coming tonight." She made me move so she could get napkins. "I figured he'd stay with his brother in Denver, come back tomorrow, and by then, I would have told you."

When she stopped moving, I handed her my full glass of wine. "Here, I filled this for you." I lifted the bottle to my lips and downed the last of it.

"Come on, let's eat. You *obviously* need food." Shelley took the empty bottle from me and set in on the counter.

Jack had been keeping a respectful distance in the living room and took Shelley's cue that our private conversation was over. Shelley put two pieces of pizza on her plate and sat at the table. Jack followed her lead.

I lagged, my appetite all but gone. The one slice I dropped on my plate might as well have been a prop. I couldn't contain a heavy sigh and trudged to the table. Shelley and Jack devoured their first slice. On to their seconds, neither spoke when I joined them. I picked at my toppings in silence, my annoyance festering. When it appeared they were almost done I took my plate to the kitchen, my pizza not even half eaten. "I'm going to bed."

"It's not even dark." Shelley either hadn't noticed the brewing tension at the table or was ignoring it.

I chose not to respond. The tightness in my chest was enough to tell me that anything I blurted out now wouldn't be worth the result. I needed Shelley in my corner. She and the brothers were the only people I had left.

# Chapter 11

The nutty aroma of fresh-brewed coffee coaxed me out of bed. I threw my hair into a messy ponytail and put on a light sweater over my pj's. There was no way I was missing out on fresh coffee, its bittersweet scent filling the hallway. I closed my eyes and let it fill me as I inhaled. A few steps from my room, I noticed how quiet it was. The living room was empty, and the drapes were closed. I stopped and held my breath so I could listen for any sign of life from the direction I had just come. Nothing.

I crept into the kitchen and opened the cupboard to retrieve a cup. I moved slow and deliberate to keep quiet. The hinge squeaked, and the mug clunked on the counter, the clatter obnoxious in the still of the apartment. When I reached for the coffee pot, I saw the time in bold blue numbers.

*Six-thirty? No wonder Shelley and Jack aren't up yet.*

I shrugged and poured the coffee. I had been awake before I smelled the coffee, so there was no way I was going back to sleep.

I went back to my room for a notebook, then went out to the balcony with my coffee. Fog still clung to places not yet touched by the sun. It made me wonder why the effects had never seemed to be an issue in the morning, even in the dead of winter, when people left for work in the dark. Perhaps it was being bundled up that kept them safe. The question lingered, so I wrote it down. The air was warm on my skin, and I was soon lost in the words as they hit the page.

Before I had finished my coffee, I heard footsteps on the balcony. I kept writing as they approached, not wanting to lose the thought I was following.

"I thought I was up early." Jack's voice made my stomach flip.

I had reconciled our situation after retreating to my room the night before. He needed a place to stay. I could either share a roof with him or turn tail and stay at my parents' house alone. Jack was much less hostile toward me than Deanna, which likely meant things would remain civil, so the comfort of Shelley's apartment won out.

"How long have you been up?" He sat in the chair beside me and sipped his coffee.

"Not long, it was about six-thirty when I came out." I kept my eyes on the page as I spoke.

"Liz." The tone in Jack's voice made me look up at him. "It's almost eight-thirty, you've been out here for two hours."

"Really? Eight-thirty?" I looked back at my notebook and scanned the page.

I flipped back through the pages, counting as I went. Twenty-three pages were filled with barely legible scribbles and a few doodles here and there. Where had I been for the last two hours? I put the notebook and pen down and took a sip of my coffee.

"Ugh, what a waste. There's nothing worse than cold coffee." I stood up and stepped toward the door.

A strange hum filled the air, and the sky went black. I whirled around to look at Jack, but the thick darkness had engulfed him. The balcony lifted under my feet, and my legs gave way. I was weightless. My arms flailed, trying to find something grab on to.

When the humming stopped, I couldn't feel myself in my body. Inside the blackness, it was still and silent. I waited for an eternity, listening for something, anything. Desperate, I called out to Jack, hoping I was not alone. No answer. I tried to move but couldn't tell if my limbs had responded. I closed my eyes and hoped this was all imagined. I braced myself, then opened my eyes. I was still in the void. I wrapped my arms tight and closed myself off to the darkness.

When I dared to open my eyes again, I had to blink hard. The dramatic change in my surroundings was blinding. My arms burned against the hot surface of the balcony. Something cold and damp lay on my forehead. I reached up and flung it away. I tilted my head and tried to focus. Shelley loomed over me, outlined by a halo of light. I shaded my eyes, and Jack came into view opposite Shelley. I felt a hand on my right shoulder.

"What happened?"

"You stood up, I think, to get a fresh cup of coffee, and fainted," Jack explained.

"How long was I out for?" I blinked and shook my head to clear it. A bolt of pain exploded behind my eyes.

"Just long enough for us to think we should call 9-1-1," Jack said.

"You didn't, did you?" I noticed Shelley had her cell phone in hand.

"You really scared us," Shelley said, still in her pajamas. Her face scrunched in apology.

"I've been up for a couple hours, and I haven't eaten yet. I just got up too fast."

Jack helped me to sit up.

"Stay there. I'll get you some water." The tone of his words confused me. While the words were firm, there was a softness to his voice that didn't fit with his general anger toward me.

"Shelley, I'm fine. Would you quit looking at me like I'm about to die."

"Then quit doing things like fainting for no reason." She made air quotes around her last two words.

Jack came back with the water. When I finished with it, he helped me stand just long enough to get me inside and onto the couch.

A few minutes later, a knock at the door told me I hadn't come to quick enough. Shelley rushed to the door. She was followed back by Kevin and a couple of his crewmates.

"Hey, Liz. How are you feeling? I heard you're having a rough morning." Kevin set a soft-sided case on the coffee table and regarded me with a small curve in one corner of his mouth, concern in his eyes.

"I'm fine, Kevin. Really. This isn't necessary."

"Well, let us at least check your vitals, and if all is good, you can do whatever you like. Humor me, though, okay?"

I couldn't say no to Kevin. I had always had a soft spot for him, so I let him do his thing.

"Okay, everything looks normal, so it's up to you what you want to do." Kevin's focus shifted. I followed it to its new location, my shoulder. "That incision site looks like it might be infected. You might want to have it examined. If it's infected, it could explain what happened this morning." He eyed me. The expression on his face this time was much more severe than just concern.

"If my vitals are fine, then I'm not going anywhere. Shelley and Jack overreacted, but if it happens again, I'll go to a doctor." I peeked around Kevin to the other two on his crew. "I'm sorry you got called out for nothing."

"It's not always nothing, so we're happy to respond. You rest up and quit scaring your friends."

I nodded. I felt a bit like a chastised child.

Kevin packed up his equipment.

The partner that had recorded my vitals pocketed her pen, then tore the bottom sheet off her form and left it on the coffee table. "If anything out of character happens in the next twenty-four hours, call us back or get her to an urgent care center. She seems fine now, but there could be an underlying condition, and falling could have several different aftereffects." She glanced back and forth between Shelley and Jack as she spoke.

"Okay, we're out." Kevin patted my shoulder, then stood and grabbed his bag off the table. "I'll catch up with you guys tonight after my shift."

"Thanks, Kev," Jack said. He followed the three to the door. I heard Jack and Kevin's muffled voices before the door closed but couldn't make out their words.

\*\*\*

My brain swirled, snapshots of all that had happened since I'd been back in town cycled through my head. I needed space and time to think. When I had convinced Shelley and Jack that I was okay, I went for a shower.

I closed my eyes under the hot water and let the events sequence themselves. My nightmares, changes to my wound, the voice I'd heard at the funeral, Deanna's accident, the fire at Jack's, and my fainting. I could only see one answer, one possibility. But was I being paranoid? Was it possible all these things were separate? Would I be trying to connect things if they were happening to other people or in another town?

*Let's think about this. I already don't have a choice in dealing with the house, Deanna's anger, and Jack under the same roof. My paranoia must be inflated by my grief. If I told Shelley and Jack what I was thinking, they'd probably laugh and call me crazy. They've lived here quite peacefully, so why would things get stirred up all of a sudden?*

Reason won out in the end, and I decided to let things be for now.

# EVERGREEN

***

Shelley and Jack were talking as I entered the living room. Their voices carried into the apartment from the balcony. I stopped out of view and listened for a minute.

"The deputy we talked to at the scene said it would be a few days before crews will be able to get into the building," Shelley said. "He didn't say as much, but I think he wanted to say if we didn't know where you were, you might be dead. I was starting to think the worst when I couldn't get a hold of you all afternoon."

"Sorry to have you all so worried for nothing. My brother called and asked if I wanted to meet him in Denver. He'd flown in first thing for a meeting, which got canceled, so he had the whole day free. I didn't want to interrupt our time looking at my phone, so muted it."

Neither said anything else. I heard the soft padding of feet on the balcony and started toward them. Jack stepped into the living room. I was a few steps from the door, so I paused to let him go by, then stepped into the warmth of the late morning. I sat next to Shelley and lit a cigarette.

"Liz, I'm sorry I didn't tell you about offering Jack a room. I didn't expect him last night, and I *was* going to tell you."

"I believe you, Shelley. It's just been a difficult couple of weeks, and he was the absolute last person I expected to see on your balcony."

"Why didn't you tell me you still had feelings for him?" Shelley asked.

"What? How do you ...? Who said I still have feelings for him?" I leaned forward in my seat to make sure he wasn't back in earshot.

"Deanna. You passed out when the deputy inferred Jack might be dead. Remember? Anyway, Dee told me she picked up on everything you were feeling before she even got to the scene. She felt your fear, your heartache, all of it."

"Oh. So, does everyone know or just you?"

"Just me. Why did I have to find out from her?"

"I didn't want anyone to know." I stared at the park to avoid eye contact. "A tiny part of me kind of thought if you knew how I felt you might try to use it to make me stay, to make it so I'd want to move back here when I finish up at Washburn." I took a drag and gazed at my feet. Shelley deserved better than that.

"We've been best friends for a long time, Liz. I was the one who helped you get over him when you left. Yes, I miss you like crazy all the time, and yes, I wish you would move back here, but I would never use your feelings about anything to get you to do something I know deep down you don't want to do."

"I know you wouldn't, Shelley, and I'm sorry for even thinking it, but you've gone to great lengths to get what you've wanted in the past. The last week and a half have been so difficult. I guess I've let my emotions get the better of me." I took a final drag and stubbed my smoke out in the ashtray. I looked Shelley in the eye. "Forgive me?"

"Of course, I do, because I love you, but don't ever accuse me of being so horrible again."

"Please don't say anything to him. I mean, it doesn't matter. He doesn't seem to feel the same anymore, and I'm still leaving as soon as I can get the house finished up. Let's not complicate things, okay?"

Shelley pulled her thumb and forefinger across her lips, then twisted an imaginary key at the center.

"Thank you."

# Chapter 12

The lamp on the side table was on when I woke up the next morning, or perhaps it was the light that woke me. I stared at it for a moment, confused. A journal lay open on the bed next to me.

*What the hell?*

I tried to recall anything from the night before. The three of us had watched a movie then caught the news before turning in. The top story was about the death of a man who'd been admitted to hospital with severe burns. They said he had walked about twenty minutes in the fog after his car had broken down. After that, there was nothing. I couldn't even remember coming into my room.

I picked up the journal and read the open page.

*November 13 – Shelley*

*I understand now why Friday the 13th is supposed to be such an unlucky day. We were using the cards with the Ouija board again today. So much faster for yes/no questions. She asked if we could leave the conversation and got a black card (black meant no, red meant yes). I asked if I could go and got a red card, so*

*I said goodbye. Liz asked again if she could go and got the Ace of Spades. The tip of the spade was pointing at her, and the planchette flew across the room and hit the bottom of her dresser. We all screamed and ran out of the room!*

*Jesus, what were we thinking, trying to communicate on Friday the 13th?*

I snapped the journal shut and examined the cover. My scalp tingled. The sensation crept down my body while I stared at the book.

*It can't be, it's not possible.*

My arm flung out. The book flew out of my hand and landed in the corner. I scrambled off the bed and hurried out of the room, my spine prickling.

*Shit, shit, shit. I have to tell Shelley. There's only one way this journal could keep showing up all over the place. I know I'm not imagining it.*

Shelley was sitting at the table with her coffee.

"Is Jack up yet?"

"Yes, but he's not here," Shelley said. "He got called down to the sheriff's station first thing. He's been gone for a couple of hours."

"How's he doing?" I poured myself a cup of coffee and joined her at the table.

"He seemed okay this morning. How about you? You seem a bit frazzled."

"Hmm, a little, yeah." I wasn't paying full attention to what Shelley was saying. I was preoccupied with trying to figure out what I was going to tell them. "How long did Jack figure he was going to be?"

"He didn't. What's going on? Why the sudden interest in having Jack around?"

I picked up my coffee and went to the balcony, Shelley hot on my heels. I sat down and lit a smoke, trying to stall and still working out the conversation we could no longer avoid.

"Liz, talk to me."

"It's better if I wait for Jack. I don't want to start twice." I pulled a long drag off my cigarette, one knee bouncing rapidly.

"Uh, okay." I heard the confusion in Shelley's voice. I knew she thought I was acting weird.

I finished my smoke and was about to get up to leave when Jack stepped onto the balcony.

"You were gone a while, Jack. Any news?" Shelley asked as he sat down beside her.

"No, not yet. The engineers will be doing a structural analysis tomorrow to determine whether it's safe for the fire crews to investigate."

"So, what took so long then?" Shelley probed.

I lit another cigarette and fiddled with my nails as he spoke.

"The sheriff was doing some preliminary investigating. I guess he got a tenant list from the manager yesterday. He wanted to know where I had been all day since I was unaccounted for because they had my name on a missing persons list. I imagine they are trying to rule out arson by getting alibis for all the tenants. Once I finished with the sheriff, I went to talk to the fire chief. I couldn't get a timeline, but he said he would let me know as soon as they've determined the cause. It's going to be at least a couple of days, and we won't know the extent of the damage until they get inside."

"Well, you can stay here as long as you need to," Shelley flashed a look in my direction.

"Something struck me when I saw the building," I said, hoping for a gentle segue. "You know, it was the same building that had the fire in our senior year."

Shelley shifted in her seat. "I thought you said something about that when I saw you, but you didn't elaborate. I thought I misheard you."

"I'll be right back." I sprinted to my room and grabbed the journal, then hurried back to the balcony and showed them the entry I'd read this morning.

"Is that …" Shelley's voice cut off. She reached for the journal. After a brief inspection, she gawked at me. "This is the journal you mentioned the other day, isn't it?"

I nodded.

"I thought you said it was at the house. How is it here?" Shelley handed the book back to me.

"I don't know. I woke up with it on my bed this morning, open to this entry." I flipped through the pages and handed it back to Shelley.

"Explains why you were acting so weird, sort of." She scanned the page.

"What's it got to do with the fire in my building, though?"

Shelley handed Jack the journal.

"I think if you go back a few pages, there's an entry or two about the first fire." I leaned toward him as I spoke.

He thumbed through the previous pages, scanning, then stopped and read when he found the entry.

"Okay, so it was the same building. It's just a coincidence." Jack peered up from the journal.

"I don't think it is. I think it's all connected. Shelley, you saw my scar last week. We thought I might have been bitten by something, right?"

She nodded.

I removed my cardigan to show them the latest. "I don't think I was, and I don't think this is infected. It keeps getting worse, but only after I have a dream."

"What do you mean, only after a dream?" Shelley said.

*Shit.* I ran a hand partway through my hair and pinched the back of my neck.

"You told me you didn't remember having any since you moved away. What are you not telling me?" Shelley's voice was full of animosity.

I glanced back and forth between them, then at the floor. Heat rose in my cheeks.

"They started the night I got here."

"Seriously, you kept *dreams* from me?" Shelley stood, her body rigid and eyes flashing with a mix of hurt and anger. I hadn't trusted her with a significant piece of information. My dreams had been a source of as much fascination as the twins' psychic powers. They had been somewhat prophetic, in an abstract way that we often didn't realize until after.

"Look, Shelley, I'm sorry. But what would you have said, what would you have done, if I had told you, my first morning here, I'd had a dream the night before? Be honest, because I know you would have overreacted."

116

"How many?" Shelley paced the balcony. Never a good sign.

"What?" I pulled my sweater back over my shoulders.

"How many dreams have you had?" She stopped in front of me. Her eyes dared me to withhold anything else.

"Four. Four dreams in twelve days."

"You didn't remember a dream for five years, Liz. Five years. You have a dream the very first night back in town, and you don't think it's worth sharing with me?" Shelley paced back and forth across the balcony again.

I looked at Jack. He sat stoic, with the journal in hand and a pensive look on his face. I turned back to Shelley.

"Look, whether I should have told you or not isn't the point. The dreams, the scar, the fog, and everything that has happened since I've been in town, it all feels connected. I was hoping it wasn't true. I could have written off Dee getting locked in the freezer as coincidence, but not after the fire."

"You had a dream about Deanna?" Jack asked.

I explained the nightmare I'd had, being lost in the snow and falling asleep in the cold. "I didn't know it was about Dee. I had my suspicions when Kevin told me about her accident, but I didn't want to say, unless I was sure."

"When did it first occur to you that your wound and the dreams might be connected?" Shelley asked.

"I didn't connect them until after the fire. Look, I don't know if it's possible, but I think the demon is back."

Shelley shook her head. "We've already had this discussion, Liz. We killed it right after it killed Stacey."

"I don't know how this works, but maybe we didn't *actually* kill it. Or maybe they can come back. It was a demon, Shelley, so who knows."

Jack stood between us and put his arms out. He eyed each of us.

"It doesn't matter one way or the other. We need to share this with Dee and the brothers. They deserve to know because if it *is* back, we have another fight on our hands, and we need to figure out how to stop this thing. For good this time."

***

About nine-thirty that night, I went out for a cigarette. The air was dense and moist. Lights from Denver reflected off the dark clouds which had gathered. Silhouettes of the trees in the park moved with the breeze that had kept the day fresh. With each drag of my cigarette, the blowing air seemed to gain strength. A cold gust blew a shiver up my spine and tickled the back of my neck. The supple willow branches whipped wildly, the movement of the tiny leaves sounding like a whispered warning. Another strong gust blew my hair across my face. Thunder cracked with a flash of lightning in the distance. I took a long, final drag, and stubbed out my smoke. I studied the darkening sky. I was glad to be here with Shelley and Jack instead of alone in an empty house with a violent storm looming on the horizon. Thunder rolled again, louder and longer. I took the hint, hurried inside and locked the door behind me.

The living room was empty. I started toward my room when I saw Jack come up the hall.

"Hey, Shelley said to say goodnight. She just went to bed. Said she's got a headache coming on."

"I'm not surprised. Storms have always affected her, and it looks like it's going to be a bad one."

Jack and I were alone. He gazed at me, his eyes dim. The events of the past forty-eight hours had taken the light from them. They told me how much pain he was holding. I wanted to comfort him, to tell him what I was thinking and feeling, but there was nothing I could say without giving my feelings away. I rolled my hands together, trying to find something to say.

"Liz, I don't know what's going to happen here. I don't know if the demon is back or if it's something else. But I want you to know I never stopped caring about you. The fire we had; the flame never went out for me."

I moved my gaze from him to the floor. He must be exhausted or in shock because he wasn't making sense. How could he still care when he hated me? I wanted to tell him I still cared about him but couldn't bring myself to say the words.

All of the emotions from the past few days erupted, and a tear rolled down my cheek.

"I don't know what you're trying to say, but I don't want to talk about feelings with you, Jack. You made yours pretty clear the other day."

I left him at the edge of the living room and retreated down the hall to privacy. I stood with my back against the bedroom door and fought to keep quiet while tears streamed down my cheeks. My shoulders shook. After a few moments, I darted across the room and threw myself onto the bed. I buried my face in a pillow and let it mute my sobs until I fell asleep.

# Chapter 13

I t was just before two a.m. when I woke from a dead sleep. I wasn't sure what woke me, but for once, it wasn't a nightmare. I propped myself up on my elbows and listened to the roar of the wind before getting up for a glass of water.

I inspected my wound under the harsh white light reflecting off the mirror while I waited for the water to run cold. I didn't remember having a dream, and as I suspected, there was no visible change.

Quiet descended over the building as I picked up my glass, but before I got it under the running water, a howling scream shattered the night, then a thunderous crash, unlike anything I'd heard before. Darkness and complete silence followed.

I turned off the water, then felt my way along the counter to the wall and found the light switch. I toggled it a few times.

Nothing.

I followed the layout of the room in my mind, my hands in front of me, and made my way back to the bed. I managed to find my phone on the side table, enabled the flashlight, and went in search of Shelley or Jack.

The warm glow of candlelight flickered from the living room. Shelley stood alone by the coffee table.

"What the hell was that?" I asked when I was a few feet from her.

"I don't know, but it sounded pretty damn close."

"Do you have proper flashlights?"

"Yes, and an emergency box in the front hall closet." Shelley started toward the hall. I followed with my light, so she could see what she was doing.

Jack was in the living room when we returned. Shelley passed him one of the flashlights.

"I haven't seen anything out of place," Shelley said. "So, whatever crashed, it had to be outside."

She opened the drapes covering the patio door. The normally impervious fog was much thinner than anticipated.

"The lights are just reflecting off the glass," I said. "Maybe we should go out and take a look."

"I don't know. The fog's pretty thin, but it might still burn. What do you think, Jack?"

"It might be okay. Let's cover ourselves, so we're at least somewhat protected."

We wrapped ourselves in blankets and opened the door just wide enough to see out at first. Shelley cast her light straight out then back and forth to make sure the balcony was intact.

"Okay. Ready?" she said.

We ventured out, Jack in the lead. Something had knocked out the entire grid and thrown the whole area into darkness. We swept our flashlights side to side in front of us, searching through the mist. At the edge of the balcony, we aimed our lights at the street and the park across the way.

"I can't see across to the park," Jack said. "I think the fog is thicker over there."

"We can't stay out here." Shelley was already moving toward the door. "Even thinned out like this, my face feels like it's starting to burn. We'll have to wait till morning to investigate."

Jack and I followed close behind.

Once inside, Jack and Shelley sat on the couch. Though I knew I shouldn't be outside, I needed a smoke. I stood with my back touching the glass door. I draped the blanket over my head and pushed it away from myself like a tent. I barely breathed between drags, depleting my oxygen. My whole body tingled as the nicotine coursed through me. When my head felt light, I shuffled across to the ashtray and stubbed out the butt. I hurried back and slipped through the door. As oxygen once again filled my blood, I felt the sting of a mild burn around my mouth.

Jack and Shelley were discussing sleeping arrangements. We would sleep in the living room together. Safety in numbers, none of us wanted to admit we were still rattled. We retrieved pillows from our rooms, Shelley grabbed extra blankets from the closet, and we all lay on the floor and hoped for sleep.

*** 

*It was mid-October. Jack and I were walking home from school. The crisp autumn air bit at our faces as the wind picked up and swirled leaves across the ground. A sudden gust almost knocked me over. Across the street, a power pole heaved and fell into the roadway. The tires of an oncoming car screeched in objection as the driver slammed on the brakes.*

*The severed ends of the power lines writhed in the street like snakes. One found a small puddle. It jerked away from the water and leaped through the air in our direction. Jack reached for my hand to pull me away from the violence, but it was too late.*

*The wild wire whipped and made contact with my leg. I screamed as the electricity ripped through my body, first in agony, then horror as I realized Jack was trying to pull me into his arms.*

*"Liz. Liz, it's okay," I heard Jack say as he smoothed my hair.*

*Don't touch me. You'll get electrocuted, too.*

Jack tightened his grip on me, and I felt his lips on my forehead before I could comprehend I wasn't in pain. The wind was gone. I opened my eyes to the flickering light of a single candle in Shelley's living room. I sat up and pulled away from Jack. Face to face, he put his hands on my shoulders, holding me still so he could look at me. In the dim light from a single candle, I saw a strange expression come over his face. He pulled his hand off my shoulder and drew it close so he could look at it, then leaned toward the candle, rubbing his thumb across his fingers.

"Oh, shit. Liz, you're bleeding."

Shelley came into the room with a first aid kit and knelt beside me. She set the flashlights toward my shoulder and shone the light from her phone over my wound so Jack could get a better look.

"Does it hurt?" Shelley asked. "Is that what made you scream?"

"No, I mean, yes, it does hurt, but that's not why I screamed." I hesitated, forgetting they knew about my dreams. "It was a nightmare. A power pole fell, and one of the wires hit my leg."

I winced as Jack cleaned the blood from the wound. He raised his head, and in a brief moment of eye contact, I saw something in his eyes I couldn't quite place. The expression was difficult to read in the flickering candlelight, but when he applied peroxide to the wound, I jerked away from the pain and turned my head sharply. The moment my gaze left him, I knew what the glimmer was—fear.

Jack finished cleaning and dressing my wound as gently as he could. When he was done, Shelley blew out the candles, then picked up one of the flashlights and turned it off.

"If your snow dream represents cold, what does electricity mean?" Shelley's voice was quiet. I knew she was close to sleep.

"I have no idea. Maybe it's not the electricity we need to focus on. What about the leg?" I laid back down.

"But how is a leg injury life-threatening? Isn't that what the other dreams were about, life-threatening circumstances?" Jack shut off the other two flashlights.

I couldn't keep my eyes open. Beside me, Shelley's breath was already deep and rhythmic. I tried to reply to Jack's suggestion, but my voice sounded disconnected and far away. My eyes fluttered as I struggled to keep them open. The orange glow from the single candle on the coffee table wavered. A puff of breath and the smell of wax and smoke told me Jack had blown out the candle. I exhaled to a five-count and sank into oblivion.

\*\*\*

A phone rang somewhere, but I couldn't quite place it. It sounded like Shelley's ringtone, but it was too far away. The noise continued and grew louder and closer with each ring. I blinked several times to clear my eyes and my head. I realized the phone had pulled me from sleep.

I heard Shelley talking. Her voice faded in and out. I sat up and a sharp pain pierced the area of my old wound. I peeked down and remembered how much it had changed during the night. Then I recalled the nightmare.

I glanced over to see Jack still asleep beside me, but I could tell by his movements that he was almost awake. Heavy footsteps in the hall told me Shelley was on her way back. She entered the room and dropped to her knees beside Jack and shook his shoulder.

"Jack, wake up, there's been an accident at Dave's. We gotta go."

"What?" I asked. I'd heard what she said, but I was still groggy, and it hadn't fully registered. "Who was on the phone?"

Shelley growled in frustration at having to explain. "Kevin. He said he just got a call-out to Dave's house.

Something about a fall and needing an ambulance. That's all I know. Can we go now?"

"Dave lives in a fourplex," Jack said. "Are we sure it's him? Maybe it was for one of his neighbors. I think we should wait for more information before we run out of here half-cocked."

"Yeah, okay. I'll call Kev back, see if there's anything more."

***

I wandered into the en suite, still groggy. I rubbed my eyes and peeled off the bandage Jack had placed on me last night. I inspected the gauze, then rotated it over and over in my hand. Confused, I called out.

"Shelley!" I left the bathroom. My pace quickened as I stepped from my room. About three feet down the hall, my gaze locked on the bandage in my hand, I ran into Jack. He grabbed both my arms just below my shoulders and eased me backward to arm's length and stared at me.

"What's wrong? Is it your shoulder?"

Shelley was right behind him and peered over his shoulder.

I shook my head, unable to speak, and held up the gauze for them to see. I flipped it over to show them both sides.

"Is that the bandage from last night?" I heard the confusion in Shelley's voice.

"That's not possible," Jack said. "You *were* bleeding, I'm sure of it. My hand was wet when I pulled it away from your wound, I swear it."

127

Shelley headed back down the hall and returned with a towel in her hand.

"Jack, look." Shelley held it out for us to see, shock in her voice and on her face. "I know it was by candlelight, and I know it was two in the morning, but I swear I saw blood on this towel."

"What the hell is going on?" My voice had returned.

"I think it's the demon, or whatever it was that locked Deanna in the freezer. Something's messing with us." Jack leaned against the wall.

"Do you think the crash last night is related?" The confusion was gone from Shelley's face.

"One way to find out," I said. "Let's go see if we can find the source."

Shelley and Jack nodded.

*\*\**

Within fifteen minutes, the three of us stepped out of Shelley's building. I lit a smoke as soon as I was on the sidewalk. The warmth of the morning was a stark contrast to the cold the storm had brought. Though it wasn't even eight o'clock, the temperature was already in the seventies, and there was no trace of the fog which had prevented a search last night.

We didn't have to go far to determine what had made the noise and caused the power outage. The cause was evident as we crossed the street. The giant willow tree that stood in the corner of the park had fallen, but we couldn't tell what had toppled the tree until we were up close.

"Does that look like a lightning strike to either of you?" Jack asked.

Where the massive trunk had given way, the edges were jagged but ordered as though some giant animal had bitten right through the trunk.

"It does not look like a tree that's been brought down by a storm." Shelley ran a hand just above the surface of the tree.

"Are those claw marks?" I traced a deep cut in the bark.

"I think so," Jack said. "But I don't want to know what made them. This tree is over a hundred-years old, and the bottom has to be at least three or four feet around."

I stubbed my smoke out on a nearby rock and stuck it in my pocket, then moved back in for another look at the tree. It appeared as though some giant animal had bitten right through the trunk, and there were, what looked like claw marks, just below the break.

"You know, I was up early the other morning before all the fog had lifted, and I could have sworn I saw something down here, but when I cleared my eyes, there was nothing."

"Why didn't you say something?" Shelley asked.

"It was the morning I fainted. By the time the paramedics were gone, I had forgotten about it."

We surveyed the rest of the park from where we stood and noted that no other trees were down. The storm hadn't brought this tree down, but it had provided perfect cover for whatever did.

We were about to head back when Jack's phone rang.

"It's Kevin," he said before answering. He hit the speaker button so we could all hear.

"Hey, Kevin, was it Dave?"

"Yeah, it was. He's got a pretty bad break. We're taking him to the hospital in Denver."

"What happened?"

"One of his neighbors heard him screaming and found him lying at the bottom of the back stairwell. I'm riding in with him, so I'll keep you updated as best I can. Guys, he said he didn't fall. He said something pushed him."

The three of us shared a knowing look.

"I gotta go, guys, they're loading him up now. I'll call you later."

Jack clicked off and put his phone in his pocket.

We wandered back to Shelley's in silence.

# Chapter 14

We were only a few feet from the door at Shelley's apartment when we ran into Deanna. She threw her hands in the air as she stepped within earshot.

"What the fuck is going on, you guys?"

We all exchanged glances. Did she know what we suspected?

"Oh, come on. I've been picking up some serious shit from you three since last night."

"We were just in the park." Jack gestured over his shoulder. "There was a huge crash last night, so we came out to investigate."

Shelley rubbed her arm against an icy breeze that whipped around us. "We were just on our way back upstairs. We can talk there."

The wind was icy compared to the air. I shaded my eyes and searched for dark clouds in the clear sky.

Deanna stretched her arm out toward the building. "After you, then."

Shelley stepped forward and unlocked the door. The rest of us proceeded to the elevator while she made sure the door closed behind her.

\*\*\*

"So, what's going on with you three?" Deanna asked once we were back in Shelley's apartment.

Jack and I folded blankets to make room to sit in the living room. I hesitated, not sure where to begin. There was so much to tell her.

"It's weird, Dee." Shelley moved the pillows to the edge of the hall. "Think about it. You're sensing again, Liz is remembering dreams, and the shit that's happened recently. You got locked in the freezer, Jack's apartment building was on fire, now Dave falls down the stairs and breaks his leg. All in the space of what, a week at most. This town hasn't seen this much action since ..." Shelley broke off mid-sentence.

It was the first time all of the incidents had been mentioned together, and the timeline was so short. The four of us stared at each other for a minute as it sunk in.

"Oh, shit," Deanna said.

The bottom fell out of my stomach, and I watched the color drain from the faces around me.

Shelley grabbed a bottle from the cupboard and poured four glasses. "I know it's early, but does anyone else want one?"

I nodded. Shelley poured, and we all shot the caramel-colored alcohol without a word. Shelley refilled the glasses. The four of us moved to the living room and sat down in unison.

"It's starting again, and I think it started with me getting back to town," I said, mostly to Deanna. I swirled my glass before taking a drink.

"I don't know about when, but I think you're right, Liz, it has started again," Deanna said. "There's never been a single ghost report at the diner, but there was *something* there the day I got locked in the freezer. I haven't felt anything there since. Looking at in hindsight, I think I was attacked."

"As much as I hate to admit it," Shelley said, "this *has* all happened since Liz got here."

"You're right." Deanna nodded. "Liz, I know there's more, I've been getting shots of anxiety from you all week, but I don't know why."

"Shelley mentioned that I've been remembering dreams, but the thing is, I haven't remembered a single dream since I left. I started remembering them the night I got here. I had a nightmare about the battle, and I've had four dreams since, which is why I think this started with me coming back."

I stood and pulled off my T-shirt.

"And then there's this ..." I pulled the dressing off my shoulder to expose my wound.

Deanna gasped, and her eyes widened. "Tell me that's not what I think, please tell me you have a new wound in the same place."

I shook my head.

"With each dream I have, it gets a bit worse." I felt my throat tighten.

"The strangest thing happened last night. The three of us were sleeping in here after the power went out, and Liz woke up screaming in the middle of the night. I grabbed her shoulders to calm her down, and when I pulled my hand away, it was covered in blood." Jack sipped from his glass, then turned his crystal blue eyes toward me.

"Yet, this morning, there was no sign I had been bleeding. The towel Jack used to clean the wound and the dressing he put on were both clean. Not a drop of blood on either of them." I emptied my glass and set in on the coffee table.

We gave Deanna a moment to process.

"Your dreams are vivid, like before, aren't they?" Deanna asked.

"Yes." I told her about the dreams in as much detail as I could remember, which turned out to be a lot.

"The dreams are warnings. Cryptic and vague, but something we should paying attention to." Deanna said.

"And Dee, the fire at my apartment–it's the same building as before." The color in Jack's face had faded since we'd started talking, and now he almost looked sick.

"I have a feeling this is going to get ugly. Do Dave and Kevin know any of this?" Deanna asked.

"No, I don't think so," Shelley said. "Certainly not about Liz's dreams or her wound. We haven't had a chance to tell them yet. Whether either of them has put the timeline together, I can't say."

"Kevin said Dave was adamant he'd been pushed down the stairs," Jack said. "So, I'm sure they figure something is going on."

Deanna didn't hang around long after our conversation.

\*\*\*

The three of us spent most of the day rehashing the events of the past several days. When we'd been over all the reasons the demon couldn't be back, we scrounged for food in Shelley's fridge.

While we ate, all the reasons why the demon must be back circled the table. Then we drank again, certain but still terrified over the prospect.

About three in the afternoon, Shelley's phone rang.

She grabbed it. "Hey, Kevin." Her eyes darted to me, then Jack. "Yes, we're here, and we're not going anywhere." She paused. "Okay, I'll let them know. Are you going to text Dee, or should I?" Shelley glanced away. "Sounds good. See you tomorrow morning."

Shelley hung up, then tapped at her phone for several seconds before putting it back on the table beside her. "Dave doesn't need surgery, thank God, and they're heading home soon. They have him on some really good pain killers right now, so he's pretty out of it. He keeps telling Kev we all need to talk, though, so they want to meet tomorrow morning. I texted Dee to let her know."

\*\*\*

When I entered the kitchen for coffee the next morning, Deanna had already arrived and was sitting at the bar.

"Hey, did you leave this on the counter?" Shelley held up the journal I had shown her a couple of days ago.

"I guess I did."

"Where did you get this?" Deanna asked.

"I have no idea. I first saw it in the spare room, then tucked behind a bunch of books in Dad's office. Thursday morning, it was open on my bed." I joined the girls at the bar. Dee handed the book over, and I flipped through to the page that was open when I'd last seen it.

"Yeah, I remember that night, it was so weird." Deanna tapped the page and spoke without lifting her eyes. "A shadow passed in front of the window at the same time the planchette went flying. Scared the shit out of me."

I grabbed my cigarettes and went out to the balcony. I stood at the railing and stared at the park. I inhaled, pulling the nicotine deep into my lungs, and held my breath for a minute. As I let the smoke out, the drug flowed into my system and provided a temporary numbness.

The sun warmed my body, and I tilted my head back to raise my face toward the sky.

A few minutes later, I heard footsteps coming up behind me.

"You okay?" Jack asked, his voice quiet and unobtrusive.

I shrugged and shook my head. "I made a huge mistake staying here after the funeral. All I wanted to do was pack up the house so I could sell it. Maybe spend a few extra days with Shelley." I tried to avoid his eyes, but the deep, lapis blue pulled me in.

"I know you didn't want to come back, and I'm sorry it was under such horrible circumstances, but I'm glad you're here."

"What do mean, you're glad? You told me you hated me the other day."

"Since then, I also told you that I still feel the flame we had. I meant what I said at your place, but it wasn't because I hate you. It was because I love you. I have always loved you."

"Jack, please. I don't want to hear this. Not now. I can't. This was supposed to be a quick trip to bury my parents, but all this shit started up again, and now I can't leave." Tears spilled over and ran down my cheeks.

Jack took a step closer and wiped the tears with his thumb. I closed my eyes and leaned into the touch I remembered so well. For a brief moment, time stopped, and all the darkness on my soul was gone.

Shelley's voice interrupted, and my stress slammed back into my chest. I stepped back from Jack's hand and wiped at the rest of the tears.

"Kevin called. We can head over any time. Are you guys ready?"

"Not by a long shot." I put out my cigarette and wiped at any tears, still trying to betray me. I glanced at Jack. "But what choice do we have?"

I followed Jack inside. I grabbed what I needed, and the four of us left for Kevin's.

# Chapter 15

"Thanks for coming, guys." Kevin ushered us into the living room of his ground level basement suite. "I brought Dave back here so he wouldn't have to deal with stairs for a while."

We filed into the room, which was brighter than I expected, and found seats on the well-used sofa and chairs.

As soon as we were all sitting down, Dave spoke up.

"My fall yesterday wasn't an accident. I was attacked. I was led out of my apartment into almost complete blackness, which I don't think was natural, and then pushed down the stairs."

"What do you mean, 'led' out of your apartment?" Jack asked.

"The power was out, and my phone was dead, so I have no idea what time it was, but there was light in my apartment, so I figured I was late for work. I got ready and left. The hallway was dark, way too dark for how light it was in my apartment. So, either the hallway was artificially darkened, or my apartment was unnaturally lit."

"You said you were pushed. Did you see anyone?" Kevin asked.

"No, but I'm pretty sure it wasn't a who. It got cold right before it happened. I felt a rush of wind go past me and, if it had been a person, I would have heard footsteps on that floor. It squeaks so bad. There's no way you could sneak up on someone."

"There's something not right about it." Kevin peered up from his coffee cup. "The neighbor who found you called it in just before seven a.m. I've been in that hallway at that time, and there's plenty of light."

Deanna leaned forward in her chair.

"Getting locked in the freezer was no accident, either. There was a presence in the diner that morning. I smudged the whole place, but it didn't work, because something had to have moved the oil pail that holds the door open. No way it moved on its own."

Jack cleared his throat. "I don't think the fire at my apartment was an accidental occurrence, either. The cause hasn't been determined yet, but I got a call from the fire chief last night. The fire originated in the center of my apartment."

"I found a journal from our senior year," I said. "It has an entry about an apartment fire. It was the same building." I reached into my purse and pulled out the journal to show Dave and Kevin.

"Oh, shit, you're right," Kevin said. "That was the same building. If I remember correctly, the fire started in the center of the same apartment."

"That's an awful lot of shit happening in one week," Dave said. "This is Evergreen, that much doesn't happen in a year."

"It's not just repeated incidents." Shelley spoke for the first time since we'd sat down. "Liz and Dee's 'abilities' have come back, too."

"What do you mean?" Dave shifted in his spot. His face scrunched up in pain. "Pills, please, Kev."

"I haven't remembered a single dream in the five years I've been gone," I said. "Not one. The night I got into town, I had a nightmare. Since then, I've had four more, three of them were premonitions, or at least they would have been if I'd been paying more attention." I stood and took off my sweater, revealing the bandage on my shoulder. "I've been a bit preoccupied with this." I peeled away the gauze and tape and let the rest of my friends see my wound. Dave was the only person who hadn't seen it. Confusion replaced the look of pain on his face. "When I got here last Friday night, this was just a scar, one I've had for five years. Every time I have a dream, it gets a worse."

Deanna jumped in. "I'm sure Kevin told you it was my aunt who called 9-1-1 when I was locked in the freezer. Did you wonder how she could've known or why I didn't just call in myself?"

Dave nodded. "Yea, I did wonder."

"I didn't have any service in the freezer, but I somehow managed to contact her telepathically. I haven't had any telepathic or empathic ability since shortly after Stacey died. Add it all up, you guys. Liz's dreams and scar, my abilities, our accidents." Deanna made air quotes around the word accidents. "It's hard to accept, but do any of you believe this is all just coincidence? Things *have* started again."

Shelley had barely said a word during this whole thing. "So, what do we do? If we didn't stop this thing before, how are we supposed to stop it now?"

Dave popped a couple of pills and swallowed a mouthful of water. "Shelley's right. We thought we killed it, right? If it's back, then we didn't. We're already down a person, two if you count me. Not like I'd be much good in a fight."

Kevin and Jack both nodded in agreement. They were all right. We needed to make sure we knew what we were doing this time. We couldn't risk this thing coming back again and again.

"Look, we'll deal with things as they come," Deanna said. "Liz, maybe you and Shelley should do some research, see if we can figure out what this demon is, and if there's a way to get rid of it for good. My aunts might know something. Stacey and I used to hear stories about this kind of thing as kids. We'd sneak downstairs after bedtime and listen to the eldest tell the others stories about our ancestors." She pointed a finger at the ceiling and waved it once. "And there's a library in the house we were never allowed to go in. I think I should take a look."

"We all need to be alert and careful," Shelley said. "Any of us could be next."

***

We dropped Dee at her place, then went to the library. Jack took the car so he could run some errands while we started our research.

The library was cool and dim after the bright summer morning. We hurried to the reference section at the back of the large building. When we located a computer, we shared a hesitant look before entering our search.

Demonology.

Shelley glanced around, then hit enter.

"Holy shit! I didn't realize there would be so many books on this stuff. How the hell are we going to figure this out before we all die?"

"I don't know." I stared over her shoulder at the screen and paid attention to the location as she scrolled through the titles. "It looks like they are all in the same place, though, so let's just go and pull a bunch of books and see if we can find any with pictures. If we can find a picture of it, maybe we can get a name or something and then find a way to kill it from there." I dropped my voice to a whisper as someone approached.

"Do you need some help finding something?"

I was shaking my head when Shelley piped up.

"Yes. We're doing a research paper for one of our classes. Would you be able to show us some of these books?"

The librarian stepped closer and peeked at the screen. "That is some pretty dark material. I hope neither of you scares easily." I caught a strange gleam in his eye just before he stepped away and started back the way he'd come. "Follow me, ladies."

He led us to a wall of books beneath a large second-story window. "We don't allow these books to leave the library, but you can sit at a table over there. You're welcome to take notes, but no photocopies are allowed, either. Some of these volumes are quite rare and delicate. I hope you find what you're looking for."

"Thank you," Shelley said.

When he was out of sight, we pulled several intriguing titles off the shelf and made our way to the table, each with an armload of books.

About half an hour later, Shelley pulled out her phone and took pictures of several pages. I shot her a look of warning.

"What? He said no photocopies, he didn't say anything about no pictures."

I shook my head, but she was right. I took out my phone and flipped a few more pages.

"Shelley, look at this." I snapped a picture.

"That's it, I'm sure of it. That's the one." We took a couple of pictures of the covers and several pages before and after the image I'd found, then put the books back and left the library. As soon as we were outside, Shelley called Jack to come and pick us up.

I lit a smoke and paced the sidewalk while we waited.

"I can't believe there's a book with a picture of that thing in it. How old was that book?"

I scrolled through the pictures I'd taken. "Would you believe the sixteen hundreds?"

***

When we got back to Shelley's, we sat at the table with Jack and conferenced Dave, Kevin, and Deanna on speaker. Shelley and I told the others what we'd found and that we had a name for our enemy.

143

"That's great news," Deanna said. "And my aunts will be able to help us a lot more than I thought. Stacey and I should have come to them in high school. She might still be alive if we had."

"What did you find out, Dee?" Shelley asked. "How could they have helped Stacey?"

"Not just Stacey, all of us. Look, there's a lot to share, so I don't want to get into it over the phone. My aunts have more to talk to me about tonight, and they want you all to come out tomorrow so that they can explain in person."

"Okay, let us know what time, we'll be there," Jack said.

"Why don't you come out around eleven? We'll talk over lunch."

\*\*\*

We all needed something to take our minds off what was happening, so after dinner, Shelley found an old movie on TV, a comedy, I think. Something about Bueller. I sat staring blankly at the screen, knocking back a few drinks.

By ten, I was exhausted and more than a little drunk. Shelley had put on the late local news, partly I thought to see if anything was happening which might be connected. The headline caught my attention.

"... died of burns sustained after being out after dark. Doctors have been unable to determine the exact cause of the burns, but believe they are related to the cases they've seen recently and to several burn-related deaths when the nightly fog first appeared in Evergreen several years ago. The number of these burn cases has increased exponentially over the past two weeks, and town officials have once again considered re-instituting a mandatory curfew."

I got up and staggered out to the balcony for a cigarette.

A fresh breeze swept up and blew away some of my stress. I stood, one hand on the railing with my eyes closed, inhaling first a breath of fresh air then a drag off my cigarette. I held it longer than normal, letting the tingle of a slight high fill my body before releasing the smoke out slowly through my nose. I lingered a few more minutes at the railing with my eyes closed, enjoying the breeze and fresh air. I let it clear my mind before taking a final long, numbing drag, then put out my smoke.

I said goodnight as I staggered through the living room without stopping. I didn't want to talk about the news. I just wanted to sleep.

I flopped onto the oversized bed, not bothering to change or get under the covers. Sleep took me quickly, dragging me into the abyss.

# Chapter 16

I woke with a start, cold beads of sweat forming on my forehead, my heart racing in my chest, intense pain in my shoulder.

I felt the dream still close around me, and when I blinked, I saw the wreckage of the single car on the back of my eyelids. The carnage was unthinkable. Two lifeless bodies lay on either side of an incredible path of torn and twisted metal.

I shook my head to rid my mind of the images and forced myself to breathe deep enough to bring my heartrate down. Pain shot through my wound and arm when I lifted it to wipe my forehead. My other hand grasped it, and I felt tears form. I hung my head for a moment and waited through rugged breaths for the pain to ease. When it didn't, I threw back the covers with my right hand and made my way to the bathroom. The bandage I had placed the night before was dotted with red spots along the line of my wound. I gritted my teeth as I pulled off the dressing, trying not to yell in pain. It wasn't light out yet, and I didn't want to wake Shelley or Jack.

The wound wept, and there was puss in some spots. I grabbed a clean cloth, doused it with peroxide, and dabbed at the yawning cut. I cleaned away the puss as best I could before pouring the peroxide over the opening. The pain got the better of me, and a yelp escaped my lips.

I gripped the edge of the counter with my teeth clenched while I waited for the bubbles to stop forming. I poured a bit more peroxide and again waited for the bubbles to dissipate. There were fewer this time, but as I waited, I noticed Shelley's reflection beside mine. I jumped, and another bolt of pain shot through me.

I grimaced as much from the pain as from seeing Shelley out of bed. "Sorry, I didn't mean to wake you."

"It's okay. I wasn't asleep. I've been tossing and turning for a while now." Shelley washed her hands and prepared to take over cleaning my wound.

"It looks bad. This is the biggest change yet, isn't it?" Shelley kept me engaged as she poured peroxide.

"Yes," I replied through tight lips as the bubbles worked to clean the infection.

"Was there a dream, too?" Shelley waited for my response before dabbing at the wound again.

"Yes, the worst one I've had."

"It won't be long now before the shit hits the fan. I hope Dee's aunts have a way for us to end this." Shelley took half a step back to get a better look at my wound. "I think I should put a couple of steri-strips on that before we cover it." She left the bathroom and returned with a first aid kit.

She applied some antibiotic ointment and removed the excess with cotton swabs before affixing the steri-strips. She put a dressing on to protect my clothes.

"That should prevent it from opening any more, but if not, we're going to have to call Kevin, see if he can put in a stitch or two, or consider taking you to a doctor."

I nodded. The stinging in my shoulder was now a moderate throbbing.

We went out to the living room without a word, wrapped ourselves in throws, and flopped onto the couch.

"Did you see the accident scene, from my parents' accident, I mean?"

"No, none of us did. The police had the road closed off for quite a distance. No one could even get close. Why do you ask?"

"Just the dream I had. It was a single-car accident, but the wreckage was like nothing I've ever heard of."

I recounted the scene from my dream while we sat waiting for the sun to rise.

Shelley sat quiet, I assumed in contemplation, once I had finished my story.

"Shelley, what are you thinking?"

"Just trying to figure out what it might mean. Why would you dream about your parents' accident? Your dreams usually tell us something, what could a dream about their death be telling us?"

"Not all of the dreams have been predictive. There were one or two that were more similar to memories than anything else."

"But no one saw the accident scene, Liz, so how could it have been a memory? It doesn't make sense."

"I couldn't see the faces on the bodies, so I guess it might not have been my parents. I just assumed it was since there was only one car, and it was so badly damaged."

"I'm not sure how we can prepare against a car accident." Shelley got up and peeked between the drapes. She pulled them open to reveal beautiful orange and pink hues above the layer of fog that still held the town prisoner. She faced me with a grave expression.

"Red sky in morning, better take warning."

\*\*\*

Deanna's aunts were already gathered under an open-sided tent when we arrived. A small feast was spread out on a low table in the center of a large circle of thick cushions.

"Dee, are all these women your aunts?" I asked.

"No. I used to think so, but only Maria is my relative."

A short woman with long red and blond hair, who appeared to be in her fifties, approached me.

"Elizabeth Porter, how nice to see you, dear." The woman pulled me in and hugged me. "I was so sorry to hear about your parents' passing. You must miss them very much."

"Thank you, Maria. It's nice to you again." I stepped back and offered the warmest smile I could muster.

"Come, everyone, get some food and sit with the sisters and me. We have much to discuss." Maria waved an arm in a broad arc as she turned, then led the way.

We did as Maria instructed, mixing in with the ten other women Deanna called aunts, most of whom I'd never met.

"The other day, I brought the journal you found here for my aunts to look through, hoping they could find something that might help us with our problem." Deanna spoke to all of us, though her eyes were on me.

Maria stood at one end of the circle with a book in her hand. I couldn't see a pentagram on the cover, but my gut told me it was our journal.

"Deanna has told us about what happened in high school. That you faced a demon and that you fear it may have come back. Before we talk about that, we want to share a secret with you all. You know us as Deanna's aunts. That is true of me, but not the rest of the women you see here today."

I scanned the faces of the women in the circle. There were just a few that I recognized. None bared any resemblance to Deanna or each other.

"We call each other 'sister' as those before us have, but our relationship is built on something more substantial than blood. We, like our mothers before us, have vowed our lives to one another and the Mother before all else. We are bound to our coven for all our days."

None of my friends spoke. Questions were visible on each of their faces, except Deanna—her questions had already been answered.

EVERGREEN

"We're witches," Deanna said. "That's where my telepathy and empathic abilities come from, where Stacey's telekinesis came from. Each of the sisters has a unique ability, and working together, we can cast spells. Real magic. Protection spells, banishing spells, binding spells. Stacey and I were never told any of this because when we were little, we didn't show any signs of the gifts, which, after some research, it turns out is normal for twins. After our mother died, my aunts thought maybe by staying here and letting us live normal lives, we could get away from the life this family has had to lead. After Stacey and I developed our gift, they were going to tell us everything, but when Stacey died, my gift stopped, and they decided there was no point in telling me about any of it. Of course, at the time, they didn't know about the demon." She turned her attention back to Maria, who now held up the book in her hand.

"As for your current situation, we think our coven has dealt with this at least once before. It may even be the reason we settled here in the first place. I know from the entries in this journal, the first time you used the Ouija was uneventful for you girls, however, I believe it was enough to wake the demon. The next time the board was brought to Elizabeth's property, the demon gained enough strength to send its energy into our world."

Maria glanced from one side of the circle to the other. "We believe that was the night the fog first descended. Then each time the board was used, the demon's strength grew. It did awful things in this town,

151

things you've seen repeated these past two weeks until, at last, you faced it in battle."

A breeze whipped across the yard and sent a shiver up my spine. The hair on my arms and neck stood up. I scanned the area, unable to find the source of my discomfort.

"You okay, Liz?" Jack wrapped an arm around my shoulder.

"Yes, just a chill." I gave him a little smile to reassure him, then refocused my attention on Maria.

"Somehow, you managed to beat the demon back and force it into a sort of dormancy. The fight was costly, as you all know. Some of you were injured, and we lost our dear Stacey. In the process, Elizabeth, you were gravely wounded, and we believe the demon left a part of itself within you. It has been dormant for several years, but it's obvious to us, as I'm sure it is to all of you, that the demon has woken. Like before, it is not strong enough to break free, but it has regained enough power to send its energy out to cause harm. We believe it won't be long before the demon is strong enough to take physical form." Maria turned her head and extended her arm toward the woman next to her. "Sister Raven."

"We believe this is why none of the recent attacks on you have been lethal. The demon's energy has only been strong enough to manipulate you into danger, not strong enough to kill you. If it had been loose, as it was before, chances are at least one of you would not be here now, maybe none of you. Deanna tells us you believe you have this demon's name. If the name truly does belong to this monster, then we can use its known weaknesses to defeat it." Sister Raven's gaze settled on me.

"We found a picture of the creature we fought," Shelley said. "The name under it in the books we found was Kafzefoni." Shelley stood and showed Maria the photo she'd taken at the library.

"We have a large library," Maria said. "I'm sure we'll be able to find what we need to defeat the demon. My dears, you must be watchful in the coming days. Further attacks could come at any time, in any form. If you can, leave no one alone."

There wasn't much for us to do now but wait for more instruction from the coven. We left Dee and her aunts and went home to absorb what we'd learned.

# Chapter 17

I sauntered into the kitchen and found Shelley dressed for work.

"So, no more working from home, I guess." I got myself a cup of coffee and sat down at the bar next to her.

"I got a message from my boss last night. They need an extra hand at the Colorado Springs office today, and the person who would normally go is on vacation. I'm sorry." She put her cup to her lips and tilted her head back.

"Don't be sorry. Work is work. I get it. You're pretty lucky to have a job that lets you work from home most of the time."

"So, what are you going to do today?"

"Well, I was thinking about going out to the house to get some more packing done, but since Dee's aunts don't want us to be alone, I guess I'll hang around here."

"Why don't you see if Jack will go with you. I don't think he's going back to work yet. I'm sure he wouldn't mind." The gleam in her eye flickered.

"What's that about?"

"What?"

"That look. The one that says you're either up to something or know something no one else does."

"I saw Jack put his arm around you at the coven meeting yesterday. I didn't know you two were getting so cozy."

"We're not. I was cold, that's all."

"Okay, okay. No need to get testy."

"Sorry." I took a tentative sip from my cup. "I don't think I slept well, and I'm a bit rattled after yesterday. You don't seem to be, though."

Shelley shrugged. "Demons are real, why not witches. It even kind of makes sense when you think about it. The fact that Dee is, and Stacey was, a witch explains a lot, don't you think? I mean, who has and lives with eleven aunts."

"I guess you're right. Look, be careful today, okay. Can you call me when you get to work?"

"Yes, Mom." She got up from her seat and gave me a sideways hug. "I gotta go. Good luck with whatever you decide to do today."

I took my coffee out to the balcony. The day was gray and much cooler than average. The air was thick and humid, making my skin feel sticky even without the heat. Goosebumps raised on my arms and made me shiver. I opted for coffee on the couch instead.

***

"Thanks for packing the tools in the garage, Jack." I said.

He unlocked the door to Shelley's apartment and waited for me to go in.

"I'm sorry I had to cut it short, but with any luck, the fire chief has news for me. I'm gonna have a quick shower and head out."

I nodded as he sauntered down the hall to his room. The morning clouds and threat of rain had dissipated, so I found a book and my usual chair on the balcony.

Not five minutes after Jack left, my phone rang.

"Shelley, hey. Are you on your way home already?"

"Liz, I'm so glad you answered. No one else is picking up."

"You sound stressed. What's going on?"

"My car broke down, and I'm stuck on the tracks, the old tracks. The car won't start, and the doors won't open." I heard thumping through the phone.

"Have you tried the windows?"

"They won't go down. Nothing's working. I just had this fucking thing serviced, and this is what happens?" I heard the frustration in her voice turn to anger.

"Okay, those tracks are abandoned, right. So, you've got all the time in the world."

I heard her take a deep breath and let it out slowly. "You're right. Is Jack around, maybe he can come and help me."

"He just left to go see the fire chief."

"Shit. I've tried Kevin twice, and he's not answering. I can't call Dave, and I don't think either you or Dee can help with this." Shelley's voice sounded panicked.

"Hold on. I'm gonna put you on conference and try Kevin."

I dialed, and Kevin answered on the second ring.

"Sure, answer for Liz, but not me."

Kevin chuckled. "Sorry, Shell. Timing is everything, and Liz's was better than yours."

"Kev, can you get down to the south road and find Shelley? She's stuck on the old tracks."

Shelley jumped in. "What's your ETA? I can't get the doors or windows to open, and it's already getting hot in here."

"I'm out that way on a job. I'll be there in less than ten minutes."

"Great, thanks, Kev. You're the best."

A strange sound came through the phone.

"Hey, Kevin, what was that noise?" I asked.

"What noise?"

"Oh, God, it can't be. These tracks are abandoned." Shelley's voice hitched.

"It sounded like a train whistle through your phone. Shelley, I thought you said you were out by the *abandoned* tracks," I said.

"I am."

"Then you need to make it less than ten minutes, Kev. I can't get out, and my car won't start."

An image from my latest dream flashed through my mind, and my heart thudded in my chest. My stomach flipped inside out. I was sure I was going to be sick.

I took a deep breath to steady myself. I'd be no use to my friend if she heard the panic in my voice.

"Shelley, stay calm," Kevin said. "Do you have anything to break a window with? A sharp piece of metal or a piece of a spark plug?" Kevin spoke with a steady voice. I'd let him do the talking unless I had to.

"I don't know." I heard muffled noises, when they cleared, I realized she must have put her phone on speaker. The sounds of rummaging continued. "I can't find anything. I don't have anything metal."

"Have you tried the back doors or windows?"

Shelley huffed and grunted. It sounded like she was struggling to maneuver around out of her seat. I heard banging and guessed she was trying to kick one of the doors open. The sound of a distant train whistle sounded again, louder than before.

"Shit. These are all stuck, too, and it sounds like that train is getting closer."

I felt the cold sting of adrenaline as it coursed through me. My body started to vibrate, and my hands shook. I tightened my grip on the phone, focused on my breathing, and told Shelley to breathe again as well.

"Kevin, for God's sake, hurry."

More banging from Shelley's end.

"Shit. Shit. *Shit*."

"Shelley, I'm almost there. Hang on."

Another whistle blast. More defined than the last one. It was impossible, but there was a train on those tracks, and it was getting closer. I tried to speak, but I couldn't find my voice.

"Kevin, Kevin, help me." Shelley's voice erupted through the speaker.

Muted thuds told me she was pounding on a window. The distant train whistle blew again, louder still.

I was rigid with fear. How could I hear a train whistle on a set of abandoned railway tracks?

Kevin's voice crackled through my phone, muffled by Shelley's windows.

The train whistled again, louder, closer.

I heard a light thud then the roar of an engine.

"Shelley?" I shouted. "Kevin? What was that?"

"He's trying to push me off the tracks. It's not working. Why isn't it working?" She screamed, and I heard what sounded like pounding on the window again. "Unnnh, fucking open, you piece of shit door." I heard fear and fury in my best friend's voice. "Kevin, what is that?"

Muffled noises again, Shelley must be moving around. Another blast of the train's whistle. It sounded so close.

I heard a loud thud, then another. The train whistle blasted. Glass smashed.

"Now, come on! *Shelley*!" Kevin's voice came through as loud as if he was standing right next to me.

A thunderous crash and the screeching of metal came through my phone's speaker, then silence.

My whole body went numb. Bile rose into my throat. I swallowed hard to keep from being sick.

"Nooooo!" My knees collapsed beneath me. I dropped my phone and knelt motionless; the carnage I had seen in my dream now vivid in my mind.

Our fight had just begun, and yet the demon had somehow just ripped two of my friends from existence in one fell swoop. How were we supposed to defeat something that could do that with such ease? We were doomed, all of us—the entire town this time.

My mind swirled with incomprehensible thoughts. Images of Jack, Deanna, and Dave flashed behind my eyes. Pain pierced my chest and spread through my throat and head. Tears flowed like a lake over the top of a dam. I was unable to move, paralyzed by shock and despair.

\*\*\*

"Liz." Jack's voice whispered to me from far away. "Liz, come on, stand up. We need to get you inside. It's pouring."

I blinked, drops of water fell from my eyelashes, and splashed in my eyes. I blinked again and felt hands on my arms, tugging at me. I shook the water from my face. Jack and Kevin were on either side of me, pulling me from my chair.

I pulled away from Kevin and slapped at his hands. He shouldn't be here, couldn't be here. I continued to flail at the vision, losing my balance and falling backward into Jack's arms.

"Hey, hey, hey. Liz, stop. It's okay. Look at me." Jack's voice was calm and soothing. My body settled in response.

"Come here."

He turned me to face him and wrapped his arms around me, one hand smoothing my sopping hair.

Jack guided me into the living room. Dave sat on the couch with his arm around a young woman in a blanket. She looked exactly like Shelley, but I had just heard her die. It couldn't be her. Did she have a sister I didn't know about? Or was it Deanna and my mind was playing tricks on me? The sliding door closed behind us, but I didn't look to see who was closing it.

Jack kept me moving toward the hall where Deanna stood waiting. I felt Jack's arms release me. Deanna took hold of me and urged me forward. I resisted, and my body arched so I could look back over my shoulder. Who was on the couch with Dave?

Dee continued to lead me down the hall. My body straightened. She guided me to my room and sat me on the edge of the bed. She lifted the bottom of my shirt. The wet fabric peeled from my skin and my mind cleared.

"Dee? What's going on? What are you all doing here? Who's Dave sitting with?"

Deanna let go of my shirt.

"I felt Shelley's panic this afternoon and called Kevin. When he didn't answer, I called Dave. He didn't know where Kev was, so when I sensed you freaking out, I picked up Dave, and we came here."

"Shelley, Kevin ... they're—" A lump filled my throat, choking off my words, and a tear ran down my cheek.

"It's okay, Liz. They're safe. Kevin and Shelley are here. He managed to get her out of the car just in time."

"Th-they're, they're alive?" A fresh torrent flooded my vision. A garbled laugh escaped me, and I leaned forward to pull Dee into a hug. "Oh, thank God."

"Ugh, you're soaked to the bone, girl."

I stood and pulled off my shirt. My left arm burned with pain and halted the motion just as my arms peaked above my head. "Aaahhh!" I recoiled from the pain, then tried again, this time removing my left arm from the bottom before pulling the soaked shirt over my head with my right.

Deanna rummaged through my laundry bag and found a zip-up hoodie. I slipped it on before she could find me a T-shirt. She stepped aside, and I dug into my laundry to find my sweats. I struggled to remove my wet shorts, then pulled on the sweatpants. A shiver ran through me now that my wet clothes were off. Deanna picked up my shirt and shorts and hung them in the bathroom to dry. We rejoined the others in the living room.

Relief washed over me when I stepped out of the hall and took sight of Shelley and Kevin. I ran to the couch and dropped into the space beside Shelley. Her arm jolted when I threw my arms around her, and a light brown liquid slopped over the rim of her cup.

"Shit, I'm sorry." I eased off and let her set her cup down, then squeezed as tight as my shoulder would allow. "I thought you were dead. I heard the crash and then nothing. I can't believe you're here." My voice cracked around the shards of glass in my throat.

Kevin stood in front of the chair beside the couch. I sprang up and hugged him around the neck before he could sit down.

"You, too. I'm so happy you're okay."

Jack walked over to me, a steaming cup in his hands. He scrutinized my face, his blue eyes full of concern, and handed me the cup.

"Just tea, you need to warm up."

I nodded and wrapped both my hands around the cup, pulling it close as if it would warm me from the outside in.

"You okay?" he asked.

"Yes, maybe." I shrugged one shoulder. "Thank you." I lifted the cup to my lips and took a small, testing sip. I licked my lips in response to the sudden heat.

Jack took a hesitant step, then lifted his arm to wrap it around me. He paused, waiting for a response. I gave a small nod of approval. He stepped in and pulled me close to share his warmth. I glanced around the room, in the safety of Jack's arms, thoughts still swirling in my head. I clenched my jaw to keep from shivering, but also to keep a cork on the conflicting emotions roiling inside.

"So, what the hell happened out there? How are you two alive?" Jack gestured to the couch, and we sat down, his arm around me like a blanket.

"There *was* a train. I saw it, but I'm still not entirely sure what happened. It just …" Shelley shrugged and turned to Kevin, who shook his head. "It just disappeared at the moment of impact."

"What about your car?" Jack asked.

"Not a mark." Kevin scratched his head and leaned back in his chair. "There is something wrong, it still wouldn't start after the train disappeared, so we had it towed, but there's not a mark on it."

"And we're fine, too," Shelley said. "I don't know what to think. I kind of feel like I'm losing it. I mean, I hallucinated a train crashing into my car."

"But I saw it, too, Shelley. I've heard of shared hallucinations but never heard of one that affects an area before. I think the demon sent a ghost train to scare you to death." Kevin rubbed the back of his neck and dropped his hand back into his lap.

"But since it's not powerful enough right now, all it could do was scare the shit out of me."

I felt a vibration through the couch and realized Shelley was still shivering.

"This is why we need to try to stick together," Dave said. "As Maria said, we are less vulnerable that way." He pulled Shelley closer and rubbed her arm.

"Agreed." Deanna set her cup on the coffee table and sat cross-legged on the floor.

# Chapter 18

The sky outside had grown dark. The downpour which had started this afternoon continued to fall in heavy sheets. I sat on the couch in Shelley's living room, Jack still at my side just as protective as he had ever been. A pizza box sat open on the living room table. Kevin was the only one still eating. I snuck out to the balcony for a smoke, still trying to process the day's events.

When I came back in, I heard Dave speaking.

"I've been doing some research, and all of the incidents we've encountered over the past two weeks happened last time, in the same order it's happening now. The outcomes differed, but the same basic incidents. The fire in Jack's building started in the same apartment. Someone was locked in the freezer at the diner, but they got out almost right away, thanks to other employees on site. A man who had lived in my apartment was admitted to hospital after falling down the back stairs but later died of a ..." Dave tapped the screen on his phone. He seemed to be looking for something. "A subdural hematoma. After today, I did a quick check, and there was a car hit by a train, but that occurred on the active tracks, and the occupants of the vehicle all died on impact."

"Shit, that's crazy." Kevin shook his head, then stood and took the stack of used paper plates to the kitchen.

"I found more. I did a search on your property, Liz. Your parents are the only ones ever listed on the land title. It was registered as a parcel almost one-hundred years ago, but no title was held until your parents purchased it in 1995."

"Seriously, the only ones *ever*? I wonder why."

"Yes, I thought about that, too," Dave said. "But I wasn't able to find anything which might explain it."

Deanna emerged from the kitchen with a glass of water in her hand. "The name we gave my aunts. They found something. This demon, Kafzefoni, is the king of something called Mazzikin. I think it's a generic term for demon." Dee sat on the floor, cross-legged, and brushed her hair over her shoulder. "The property may have sat empty on purpose. The land might have been inhabited or claimed by a Mazzik. My aunts said building on a Mazzik's land is dangerous. Over time, the need for that land to stay vacant was forgotten, and by the nineties, more tax dollars won out over anything else, and your parents were allowed to buy it."

"Oh, my God. No wonder I never felt safe when I was alone there. So, what now?"

"My aunts are working on a spell. They don't think they'll be able to destroy Kafzefoni, but they're confident they can bind it somehow, put it back to sleep."

"So, what about the rest of us?" Shelley shivered under her blanket and shifted closer to Dave.

"Hang tight for now, I guess. There's not much to do except try to stay safe."

\*\*\*

The rain stopped before everyone left. The dark sky was clear, and the night air was much warmer. I grabbed my smokes and went to the balcony. I sat on one of the chairs and covered my face with my hands. Shelley followed and took the chair beside me.

"Talk to me."

"About what?"

"Whatever it is that has you hiding."

I lit the cigarette I had been holding and slowly exhaled the first drag. "I don't know what you're talking about."

"Come on, Liz. You might be able to get away with that with some of the others, but not with me. I know you too well. Tell me."

I took another drag and gauged the look in Shelley's eye. One more drag in silence. I knew I had to tell her. She probably knew anyway.

"Every day I'm here, it gets harder to be around Jack, harder to stay away from him."

"Then why fight it?"

"Because, if I don't, I'll be hurting him again when I leave. Giving Jack hope for a future we can never have would just be cruel."

"Don't you think he should have a say in whether the two of you can be together or not?"

"Shelley, come on, I can't be with him, you know that. If we make it out of this again, I'm gone, for good this time, I'm not kidding. I mean, maybe if this had been a normal visit and all this shit wasn't happening again ..."

"That doesn't tell me why he shouldn't have a say. We're adults now, Liz, not kids just out of school. If you still love him and he still loves you, then it should be a discussion about your future, not a one-person decision."

"No. His life and his parents are here. I could never ask him to leave them, and that's what would have to happen."

"Shouldn't that be his decision to make? People leave their families all the time. It's not that strange. Think about all the people who leave to go to school overseas. Liz, I think maybe you're just afraid of letting yourself be happy. That's not even starting on how you plan to maintain the relationship you seem to have rebuilt with Deanna."

"That's not fair."

"Isn't it? You know, you're lucky she's even considering giving you a second chance. Just because I said you were a no-go topic doesn't mean I didn't understand how she felt. You hurt her deeply when you decided to cut off all contact, but it was worse that you kept talking to me."

"You're like a sister to me. How was I supposed to go through life without you?"

"Maybe the same way Dee has to live the rest of her life without her twin, her blood born sister. If you're going to run away again, consider that if you change your mind one day, it's doubtful that she will. And you know how capable she is of making people's lives miserable. That was before she knew she was a witch."

I finished my smoke, sulking. Shelley was right about most of it, and I might have to consider keeping in touch if not visiting once in a while, but I still didn't want to have that conversation with Jack.

# Chapter 19

The next morning was sunny and warmer than normal for this late in the season. I stepped on to the balcony to a symphony of birds and children's laughter floating up from the park. The day was in complete contradiction to the previous afternoon. It felt and smelled like spring. The light breeze carried the scents of myriad flowers, and I could almost hear the hum of bees zipping about.

As I sat with my coffee, I thought about Shelley's near-miss yesterday. I wondered whether the change in atmosphere today was the demon's doing. If it could produce a ghost train complete with sound and vibration, could it also control the weather?

Shelley interrupted my thoughts when she came out to join me.

"Good morning, Liz."

"Good morning. Going to work again today, I see."

"Yes. Not much of a choice, but Kevin's still working out that way, so he's going to take me in. Look, I'm sorry if I was a bit harsh last night. I just wish you would consider that Evergreen isn't so bad."

I gawked at her.

"Okay, yes, we are up against a demon for the second time in our lives, but the town itself and our friends and families are here. We could have lived anywhere and still ended up fighting this demon. What if it came after you and you weren't here with us? Would you still hate this town?"

"You have a point. I guess I just dealt with my trauma differently than the rest of you did."

"I'm not saying it's bad or wrong, but maybe you haven't dealt with it all."

A horn blared on the street below. Shelley peered over the railing and waved.

"Look, I love you, no matter what. Just think about what I've said. I'll see you tonight, okay."

Shelley hurried back inside, and a moment later, the apartment door banged shut, signaling her departure. For the second day in a row, it was going to be just Jack and me. He was another issue she would say I haven't dealt with.

I continued to mull over what Shelley had said, how she was so emotionally intact after her incident was beyond me. I'd only had to hear it through my phone, and I still didn't feel as stable as she seemed to be.

The clinking of a mug on the counter grabbed my attention.

*Jack must be up. I suppose Shelley's right. Maybe I do need to talk to him.*

It was now or never. A deep breath solidified my courage. I stood, marched across the balcony, over the threshold, and past the living room furniture. Jack was still in the kitchen.

I opened my mouth to speak, but a shimmer of light to my left caught me off guard. I twisted toward the source, but the shimmer was gone, a red blur in its place.

Reality registered too late. A jolt of pain hit me in the shoulder so sudden and severe it made me scream.

Blinding white light filled my vision as pain shot through me. The light faded as fast as it had struck, then nothing. No color, no sound, no feeling. Nothing.

\*\*\*

I opened my eyes and found myself in bed, but it wasn't my bed. The light in the room was white and harsh in contrast to the blackness I'd become accustomed to. I squinted against it. Somewhere behind me, something was beeping incessantly.

I tried to look around. My body ached and felt as though it were encased in five feet of wet sand. I resorted to scanning the room with my eyes. Jack was slumped in a chair a couple of feet away. I tried to speak, but my throat was dry, and all I managed was a cough.

Jack jolted in his seat, then raised his head and studied me. His eyes brightened, and a small smile crept across his lips. He stood and stepped to the side of the bed. He grasped one of my hands and put his other on my shoulder.

"Don't try to talk just yet. I'll let the nurse know you're awake and get you some water."

All I could do was nod.

A moment later, a nurse came in and took my vitals.

"Welcome back, Miss Porter. You gave us all quite a good scare yesterday. Your vitals are looking much better, and it looks like you've got most of your color back. I'll send your friend back in for a few minutes while I have the doctor paged."

The woman barely made it out of the room before Jack was back at my bedside.

He handed me the paper cup he held.

"They said all you can have for now is ice chips."

I did my best to smile and let Jack put the cup to my lips and shake a few chips into my mouth. I sucked on them and let them melt. The cold water soothed my raw throat as it trickled down.

Jack stood beside me. It seemed like he was about to speak when the doctor came in.

"I'm gonna go call Shelley, let her know you're awake. I'll be right back." Jack squeezed my hand, then ran his fingers through his hair as he left the room.

The man at the foot of my bed appeared close to six feet tall. His brown hair was peppered with gray. I guessed he was probably in his mid-forties. I felt much more comfortable in his care than the young nurse who had been there before.

He remained at the foot of my bed for a few minutes reading my chart then took the few steps to the side of my bed.

"Good morning, Liz. I'm Dr. Powell. I'm a thoracic surgeon, and I treated you for a severe stab wound yesterday."

"Stab wound? What happened?" My voice was raspy, and my throat ached.

"We're not entirely sure. Your boyfriend said he found you lying on the floor in a pool of blood yesterday afternoon. Judging from the wound you sustained, we believe you were attacked. Do you remember anything?"

"Yesterday?" I wrapped a hand around my aching throat.

"Yes. You sustained a stab wound just below your left shoulder. You lost a significant amount of blood, so we had to give you a transfusion. It was touch and go for a while, but we managed to keep you on this side."

I knew exactly how I had gotten the wound, but it didn't happen yesterday. I thought hard, trying to find any scrap of memory, but I was tired, and it was too far away right now.

The doctor did a couple of more tests in silence, minus a few simple instructions.

"I see your vitals are back to normal." He pulled down the top of my gown just enough to inspect my wound. He lifted the dressing and pressed around the wound site, making me grimace.

"Looks like your wound is already starting to heal. Considering how ugly it was in there, I have to say I'm surprised at how good it looks. I want you to get up and walk around your room. I'll send a nurse in to help you. If you do okay with that, I will move you out of ICU, but I am going to keep you in for at least one more day for observation."

My mind was reeling, but I nodded, razors in my throat kept me from speaking.

*What the hell happened yesterday?*

The last thing I could remember was wanting to talk to Jack just after Shelley left. After that, there was nothing. It just cut off like the end of an old movie reel.

The doctor left, and Jack returned in his wake, his phone still in hand. "Shelley and the others will be here in a while."

Jack sat in the chair he had been occupying when I woke up. He picked up my hand and held it between both of his, gazing at me solemnly.

"Liz, I thought I'd lost you for good. I know you aren't mine to lose, but God, if you'd died, I don't know what I would do." The words came out choked, and I could tell he was fighting hard to keep it together.

"It's okay if you really have moved on, Liz, but if you haven't, you need to tell me. These attacks are getting worse, and after yesterday, I fully expect at least one of us won't make it through this. I don't want you to say anything today. I want you to rest so you can get out of here." Tears rolled down his cheeks, and I could tell his anguish was worse today than it had been five years ago when I said goodbye.

"I love you. I always have, and I will do whatever it takes for us to be together if you feel the same. I mean it. If you let me back in, I will never leave you, and I will go wherever you want to be."

He lifted my hand and leaned forward. His lips brushed my skin, and he sat locked in that position with his eyes closed for several minutes. My hand was still in his when I drifted into blackness.

\*\*\*

I heard whispers and opened my eyes to see Shelley and Deanna standing next to Jack near the door of my room.

I watched as Jack left the room. Shelley wandered over.

"How are you feeling, Liz?" She filled the seat Jack had occupied. Deanna stood next to her; hands tucked into her front pockets.

"Confused mostly, and tired." I reached for the cup of ice on my table. "The doctor said I was attacked yesterday, but I don't remember anything."

"If it was the demon that attacked you, it might explain that," Deanna said. "There might not be anything to remember."

She stared at me; her eyebrows scrunched in concentration.

"What?" My voice was hoarse and raspy. It still hurt to talk. The ice chips had melted, but the water was still cold in the foam cup.

"Just reading you, there's a lot in there."

"Well, stop it."

"Fine, but only because you're in here. My aunts wanted me to check out your property, so I went out there this morning. I found an energy source coming from the woods at the north end of your property. I didn't go past the tree line, so I don't have an exact spot, but there is a malevolent presence out there. I'm pretty sure that's our demon."

"That could explain why I always feel like someone, or *something* was watching me from that area." I tipped the cup back and let the last of the melted ice trickle down my throat.

"Deanna's going to stay here today. We've decided that everyone will stay at my place for the next few days, so the rest of us are moving stuff around and making some additional space in the guest rooms. After you were attacked with Jack just feet away, we can't take any more chances. This has to be our focus, one-hundred percent right now."

Shelley hugged me goodbye, and I groaned under her pressure on my left side.

"Ooh, sorry. Too tight?"

I nodded as she straightened. Jack returned and took Shelley's place and bent down to kiss my forehead. "Think about what I said, okay. I'll be back tonight after we all get settled."

# Chapter 20

Once she was sure they were out of earshot, Deanna spoke.

"You're an emotional supermarket right now. What's going on with you and Jack? He's put his cards on the table."

I held up the empty cup and wiggled it. If she wanted me to talk, I was going to need more ice chips.

"Water or ice?"

"Ice."

Deanna huffed. "Fine, but then you're going to answer some questions."

When she came back, she repeated what she'd already asked. I sucked on a few ice chips and let the cold dull the blades in my throat.

"You could say that. Jack told me this morning that he would leave Evergreen for me."

"So, did you tell him how you feel?" She cupped her hand in her lap and leaned in with a smile on her face.

"No, I haven't had the chance. He wouldn't let me say anything. Besides, I'm not sure it changes anything."

"Why not?"

More ice. Dee regarded me expectantly.

"Quit stalling, Liz. Convince me why you shouldn't tell Jack how you feel."

"I don't want him to give up his family and his life for me. Besides, is this really the time for us to be reconciling? Don't we have bigger things to worry about right now?"

"I know what you're feeling, and some of it is founded, but here's the thing. If you're wasting energy on fighting how you feel or worrying about Jack's feelings, you're vulnerable, and you can't focus on the demon. If you're vulnerable, the rest of us will be, too, because we'll be worrying about you."

"I hadn't thought about it that way."

"I'm not the only one who can see your feelings. I told Shelley, but I know she didn't tell anyone, and both Dave and Kevin have asked me point blank. I lied, said I didn't know, wasn't sure. But they can see it, so I'm sure unless he's completely blind, Jack can, too."

I shrunk into the bed and stared at Deanna feeling sheepish.

"Tell him," she said. "Let him decide what he's willing to do, and then the two of you can decide from there. But first, you have to tell him, and you need to be one-hundred percent honest."

I shifted. The movement was two-fold. I needed to get more comfortable, but I was also pausing to take stock of what Deanna had said. She was right. I was wasting too much energy, worrying about how Jack felt, and about decisions only he could make.

I yawned. I hadn't been awake long, but it was exhausting taking all this in.

"Get some rest, I'm going to get a coffee and a magazine or something, but I won't be long."

I nodded and adjusted myself again. My eyes drooped. I didn't fight it, and before long, I was asleep and dreaming.

The dream felt so real, as most of my dreams did. But at the same time, somehow, I knew I was dreaming.

\*\*\*

*It was early winter. Shelley and I were with Deanna and Stacey at the library doing research. We had books laid out all over the table. Notebooks lay overtop and in between, wherever there was room. Several of the books had sticky notes on pages we wanted to go back to.*

*Shelley and Stacey left the table to take a break, leaving Deanna and me alone. We chatted a bit while we worked, then Dee stopped mid-sentence. When I glanced up from what I was writing, she was gone. The pen she had been writing with lay on the pad of paper where she had been sitting.*

*I scanned the area. She couldn't have gone far. I stood and moved to the other side of the table, thinking maybe she had bent to pick something up off the floor, but she wasn't there. I turned a full three-hundred-sixty degrees looking for her. She had disappeared.*

*I jogged through the library, looking for her. I had to find Shelley and Stacey, too. I had to tell them*

*Deanna was gone. Then I realized no one was in the library. All the people who had been wandering the shelves or sitting at tables were gone. Even the librarians were missing. I was alone.*

*The hairs on the back of my neck stood on end, and a chill ran down my spine. My mind told me to run, but my feet didn't seem to be listening. Instead, I slowly pivoted to face whatever was there.*

*I closed my eyes and drew in a breath to steady my nerves, which screamed at me to run the other way. I opened my eyes and saw, not the monster I expected, but a man. He didn't look much older than me. He was tall with sandy-blonde hair, and I could tell he was muscular through his shirt and jacket. He was well-groomed, too. His clothes suggested he came from money, old money.*

*He stood inches from me, smelling of warm cinnamon. He stared down at me with caramel eyes flecked with gold and a smile that would have made me melt, but there was something off about him. I just couldn't put my finger on it. My spine tingled, and despite his outward charm, I didn't want to be around this guy.*

*"It won't be long now, Liz," he said in a honeyed voice. "We'll be meeting again soon, and this time, I'll take care of your friends so they can't get between us. I won't let you get away from me this time." As he spoke, he laid his index finger on my chest just below my left shoulder. White-hot pain surged through me.*

*Before I could say or do anything, he vanished. I blinked and looked around for him even though I knew he wouldn't be there. I rubbed my eyes and blinked again.*

I was back in my hospital bed. Deanna was in the chair next to me.

"You okay?" She studied me; her eyebrows furrowed. "I got the strangest urge to run from the building, and now I'm just confused."

"I just met the demon."

# Chapter 21

I had gotten out of bed long enough for the doctor to move me out of ICU late the previous afternoon. Now I wanted out of the hospital entirely. I stood and grabbed the IV stand beside my bed.

Jack had relieved Deanna just before visiting hours ended and sat at my bedside all night.

"What are you doing?" He got to his feet and reached for me.

"Going to the bathroom. If I can't do that on my own, do you think the doctor is going to let me out of here today? I'll take it slow, I promise."

Jack stepped aside and let me through, knowing full well I was right.

I peeled back the dressing to look at the wound on my chest. It was grisly. New stitches barely held the meaty mess together, and surgical antiseptic still stained my skin. I gently rolled my shoulder and grimaced at the stiffness.

*Better not rush this too much, or I'll tear the stitches.*

Stephanie Galay

I pressed the gauze back down, lightly rubbing the tape to ensure it would stick. I flushed the toilet for good measure, then made my way back to bed. Dr. Powell was waiting for me when I opened the door.

"Good morning, Elizabeth. How are you feeling today?"

"Pretty good." I smiled, hoping it would make the words more believable.

"Your boyfriend tells me you would like to go home."

"That's right." I marched past the doctor and sat on the bed.

"Well, being up on your own is a start. Did you have any dizziness getting out of bed?" Dr. Powell flipped through my chart.

"Nope, none." I lied just a little.

"It looks like your vitals have been steady since yesterday afternoon. Let's have a look at your wound site."

I pulled my legs up on the bed and leaned against the pillows as he pushed a button, making the head of my bed flatten out a bit.

He removed the dressing, inspected it briefly, then tossed it in the garbage. He grabbed a penlight from his pocket and leaned in for a closer inspection. He pressed all around the area, noting my reactions.

"According to your chart, you haven't had any pain killers this morning. What would you say your pain level is right now?"

"My shoulder is stiff, and there's some slight throbbing, but unless it's being touched, I would say maybe three or four. Nothing I can't live with."

"Well, I don't see any reason to keep you here. Do you have someone who can stay with you for the next couple of days? I would prefer you weren't on your own, just yet."

"I won't be letting her out of my sight." Jack glanced at me, sincerity mixed with a warning flashed in his eyes.

"Your wound was a real mess inside. I've never seen anything quite like it, and I had to do a lot of cleanup, so I have you on a broad-spectrum antibiotic to prevent infection. I also want you to keep in mind that you had a blood transfusion, even though you might feel okay, your body still has a lot of healing to do. You need to take it easy for several days before you start to ease back into your normal routine. Any questions?"

"Antibiotics, blood transfusion, someone around twenty-four/seven for a few days and take it easy. Got it, and believe me, Dr. Powell, my friends aren't about to let me out of their sight until I'm ready to go back to Topeka."

"Well then, I guess I can sign your release papers. I'll send your nurse in to unhook you from all these wires and take out your IV. Here's a prescription for the antibiotic. Take care of yourself, okay?"

"I will, Dr. Powell. Thank you."

\*\*\*

Shelley's living room was full when Jack and I arrived. The furniture had been rearranged, and a mattress was propped up against one wall, which made the room look much smaller than it was.

Jack rushed past me, acting as a shield, as our friends stood in greeting.

Kevin approached first and hugged me much gentler than usual. "It's good to have you back, Liz. We were all pretty worried. Thought we'd lost you."

The rest of my friends repeated Kevin's sentiment as I made my way to the sofa to sit down. Their concern reinforced how much they all meant to me. I had grown up with them, and then we had collectively survived a literal trip through hell. That they were in this room for me today made me realize how selfish I had been when I had left. I had told myself leaving this town behind was for my survival, but my friends were all still here—they had all survived in Evergreen for the past five years. Maybe I had been wrong to leave home behind. Maybe things could work here if we were able to survive the next few days.

I sat on the right side of the sofa, legs folded beneath me, and leaned against the armrest. My shoulder throbbed, and I was surprised at how tired I was after just coming up from the car.

"Can I get you anything, Liz?" Shelley was standing over me. I hoped she was the only one who could tell how tired I was just now.

"No, thanks. I just need to rest a bit."

"You look amazing for someone who just about died two days ago." Dave hobbled over on his crutches and took the seat next to me so he could put his foot up on the coffee table. He grabbed a cushion and stuck it under his cast, both to protect the table and provide what little comfort might be possible.

"I had a blood transfusion, so I guess that helps. The surgeon said I lost a lot of blood." I stared at my hands, unexpected emotion boiling to the surface. "Jack, I owe you my life, literally. If you hadn't been here, I wouldn't have made it. The surgeon made that crystal clear."

Jack smiled and nestled himself between Dave and me.

"Do you remember anything?" Dave asked.

I shook my head. "It happened so fast. Shelley had just left. I think I was headed for the bedroom. There was a shimmer, and I got this intense pain." I put my hand over the fresh wound. "A white-hot intensity, and then everything went black. The next thing I remember is waking up in the hospital."

"It sounds like the demon is getting stronger." Shelley wrapped her arms around herself. "Dee, I thought Maria said it wasn't strong enough to do any real harm."

Deanna nodded. "She did."

Shelley waved her hand in my direction. "Well, that was a lot more than just creating a life-threatening situation. It physically attacked her without even being here."

"If it can do that, what chance do we have? Look at us. The only one who hasn't been attacked is Kevin." Dave scratched at the scruff on his chin. "Not that I'd want that to happen, Kev. Just fact."

"I know. Love you, too, bro." Kevin gave a curt upward nod.

"I dreamed about him," I said, almost under my breath.

"Dreamed about who?" Shelley asked.

"The demon. In the hospital." I eyed Deanna then shared the details with all of them.

"Did you ever dream about the demon in high school?" Kevin asked.

"No. I don't think so. I had some pretty intense dreams back then, but I don't recall ever dreaming about any demons."

I yawned and tried to stretch but recoiled as lightning radiated outward from my wound. I grimaced.

"We should let you rest," Deanna said. "My aunts are expecting us all tomorrow afternoon—if you're feeling up to it, Liz."

"Would they come here if I'm too tired?" I asked as she bent to hug me.

"If the demon has been here, it's not safe. The coven's property is under protection, though, so we'll be able to talk freely there and figure out what we're going to do to end this. I was going to stay here, but it's pretty full, so I'm going to stay with my aunts."

I nodded my understanding. "All right."

"I've got to go check on our job sites, so I'll be back later." Kevin crossed the room, bent to hug me, and whispered in my ear. "I'm glad you're still with us. Get some rest. It sounds like you're gonna need your strength sooner rather than later."

The apartment still felt full when Dee and Kevin had left.

## EVERGREEN

As soon as Kevin had the door closed, I went out to the balcony to get some fresh air. I sat down in one of the chairs, and for the first time since arriving in Evergreen, I did so without lighting a cigarette.

\*\*\*

I had just closed my eyes to absorb the heat and energy from the sun when I heard Dave come up behind me. The rhythmic, metallic sounds of his crutches clicking as they set, followed by the slight thump of a single foot hitting the balcony was unmistakable. I slowly opened my eyes and adjusted to a more upright position as I waited for Dave to take the seat next to me.

"To what do I owe the pleasure of your attention?"

"I figured misery loves company."

"Hmm, it does. How's the leg doing?"

"It's better. The pain is manageable now. The first couple of days were pretty bad. Good thing they had me on all those drugs in the hospital."

"Did you come out for the sun and fresh air, too, or is there something more?"

"Both." Dave's tone became serious with that one word. That tone was never good. Had I been in better condition, I would have bolted, but I was way too tired to try, so I braced myself for what was coming.

"You crushed him when you left, you know, Liz. He's never fully recovered from it. You were the world to him. It's been hard for him since you got back. Let me tell you, the man has hope, but it was almost

189

shattered when he saw you lying there in a pool of your own blood.

"Look, I know you left here because you were still hurting, and you were afraid, and you hated being reminded of the horrible things we faced. So, you went away, and you survived, but we all managed to survive *here*. Do you know why we survived, Liz? We had each other, and we didn't give up when things were at their darkest. Hell, Kevin literally got a second chance at life, and look at him. Happiest guy I know. Maybe it's because he doesn't remember every detail, but I am also pretty sure it's because he chooses to find those little rays of light in the darkness and holds on to them for all they're worth.

"You can hide away in Topeka and pretend like none of it ever happened if you want. You can go back there for good this time, now that you'll be done with the property. We'll all go on here together, and when things get bad, we'll face them with the support of our friends, and we'll survive and probably even be happy. For the most part, I think most of us are happy. We're scared right now, but we've been happy here. Are you happy out there on your own, Liz? Are you living or just hiding?"

I sat in my chair, somewhat stunned at Dave's candor. He had never been one to hide the truth, but he wasn't usually so pointed and brutal when he spoke. At least, that wasn't what I remembered about him.

"It was a long time ago, but I remember what it was like to love you. It may not be the same as Jack's love for you, and it has changed, but I do still love you. We all do. After it all ended in senior year, I decided that life was too short. Any day could be my last, so, when I feel strongly that someone I care about is making a mistake, I let them know. And you've been living a colossal mistake for five years, Liz. I just haven't had a chance to tell you until now.

"It's not a bad life here, Liz. I have work, I have friends and family, and I have faced the worst here and lived to talk about it. I take strength from that. What we went through does play a role in who we are, but it's really about how we deal with life afterward, moving forward instead of looking back."

I had been twirling my thumbs together, my eyes fixated on them instead of Dave. Now I ran a hand through my hair and gazed skyward, my cheeks hot with defensive hostility until I realized it wasn't Dave I was angry with.

"I never really thought about it that way. Maybe you're right, maybe I've been hiding. School makes it pretty easy to justify. I suppose having my nose buried in books hasn't been much different than burying my head in the sand, has it?"

"Not really. I have a question for you, and I want you to be completely honest with yourself when you answer this, okay? Do you still have feelings for Jack?"

"Yes, I do."

"Then you need to tell him. You didn't see him on Tuesday. The man was a mess, so, no matter what you do in the end, you need to tell him how you feel. Leaving doesn't have to be permanent, Liz. Even if you decide you can't come back here to live, what's the harm in coming back to see Jack, and the rest of us, for that matter. Look, the way I see it, if two people love each other, they should be together whatever it takes."

"I know. You're right, Dave, and I already tried to tell him. I think that's what I was going to do when I was attacked."

"See, I'd get on it. You never know when your last chance will come, and if you miss it, you will regret it."

I closed my eyes and breathed deep, trying to hold back the tears that threatened.

"One last thing. I've learned over the past few years, the only way to *find* happiness is to *choose* happiness. You get to choose how you feel about pretty much everything in life. All of these attacks, for example, you could choose to believe our group is extremely unlucky and, oh my God, four of us have almost died in the past two weeks, or you can flip the coin and realize that all four of us survived some pretty horrific accidents. It's all a choice, Liz, all of it."

Dave pushed himself up onto his crutches. "Food for thought. I still love you, no matter what, Liz. We all do, but don't miss your chance, okay." He hobbled his way across the balcony and back inside.

I leaned back in my chair and closed my eyes again. I let out a heavy sigh, unable to stop the tears from spilling over the corners of my eyes.

\*\*\*

The rest of the day went by peacefully. I napped on and off, leaving the sun-soaked balcony only to go to the bathroom. All the trauma and revelations of the past few weeks tumbled over in my mind while I was awake, and dreamless voids let my mind rest.

As the quiet afternoon eased into a calm evening, the aromas of a gourmet meal filled the apartment and drifted out to the balcony. Jack had decided to treat us all to a feast of seafood paella. Shelley came out to get me when dinner was ready.

Though the scent of simmering tomatoes, garlic, and wine had made my mouth water, I was unable to appreciate Jack's culinary efforts. Every bite was flavorless, and though I knew I had to regain my strength as soon as possible, I struggled against my diminished appetite and sense of taste to force something into my system. I was glad I had only allowed a small amount on to my plate. While the others made each bite sound orgasmic, I pushed what little I had around on my plate, dreading each mouthful.

"Anyone into watching a movie?" Dave hobbled on one crutch to take his dish to the kitchen.

"Sure, I could use the distraction." Shelley was already in the kitchen, filling the sink.

"I'm in, too." Jack stood and laid a hand on my back. "How 'bout you?"

I shook my head. My eyes felt gritty, and my head was cloudy as though I'd been up for days.

Kevin grabbed my plate and went to help Shelley with the cleanup.

I left the four of them with the cleanup and went to bed. Almost as soon as my head hit the pillow, the world around me disappeared into darkness.

# Chapter 22

I had woken before the others thanks to retiring to bed so early. I stayed in bed as long as I could, but the sun streamed in over the top of the curtains and called to me. The apartment was silent when I stepped out of my room, so I crept down the hall as quietly as possible.

I slipped a piece of paper under Jack's door on my way out to the kitchen. I made a pit stop for coffee, then snuck out to the balcony where I sat with a notebook and made a list of pros and cons about life in Evergreen.

We had just over an hour before we needed to leave to meet with Deanna and her coven when I heard the sliding door open.

I watched Jack step into the warm morning air. His chocolate hair, still wet from a shower, glistened in the sunlight. He sat next to me and held out a folded piece of paper.

"You wanted to talk?"

"Yeah." I closed the notebook, clipped the pen to the cover, and set it beside me, my gaze never leaving him.

At first, Jack appeared nonchalant, but his eyes held a pain that mirrored my own. I found myself unable or perhaps unwilling to maintain the emotional defense I had built up, feeling it crumble under his stare.

Jack spoke first. "I know the current housing situation is not what you would prefer, but we need to be safe. I could have gone to stay with Dave and Kevin instead, and I might have, but after Tuesday, I mean, it probably doesn't make much difference. I was right there, and I couldn't stop it from happening. I thought you were already dead. There was so much blood, so fast. I don't know what I would have done if I'd, I mean if *we* had lost you."

"Okay, Jack."

"Liz, I love you. I've told you that before, and I will do all I can to protect you. Wait, what did you say?"

I laughed in spite of myself.

"I said, okay, Jack. I can't fight you anymore. I can't fight us anymore. I never stopped loving you either. I just put it away. I told myself that if I made a life somewhere else, that you would just be a memory, another piece that I would eventually forget, and I would find someone and be happy."

Jack's eyes brightened as I spoke.

"It has been pointed out to me that I may not be as happy in Topeka as I have been telling myself. These last few weeks have made me realize how much I've missed all of you and that I don't have any true friends in Topeka. I'm pretty sure if I leave there, I won't be missed. The point is, I've been lying to myself for a long time, and I can't do it anymore. I love you, Jack. I always have."

Jack grabbed my hand. He tried to pull me from my chair, but I resisted. I raised a finger on my free hand.

"Please, let me finish. Some unsolicited advice the past few days urged me to admit how I feel about you, but I'm not sure sharing that with you changes anything. I still don't know that we can have a future together, because I don't know if I can come back to Evergreen after I finish my degree."

"You don't have to come back here. I would go wherever you need to be. I just can't lose you again."

"If we both survive what's coming, I'm willing to have a conversation about it this time, but we need to focus on destroying the demon, or whatever it is we're able to do to it."

Jack knelt beside my chair and placed a hand on either side of my face. He wrapped his fingers behind my ears and stared into my eyes, the pain all but gone from his eyes. With the love that had always been there, I saw hope instead of sorrow. He lingered for a moment then kissed me as if making up for the last five years.

When he released me, I saw the streak left by a tear that ran from the corner of his eye to his chin.

"I don't want to go into this fight with questions between us. I know the stakes, Liz. We'll discuss a future if we both survive, I'll concede that, but in the meantime, if we both feel the same way, I don't see why we should deny ourselves a sliver of happiness now."

"Let me think about it, okay." The words escaped my lips so softly I almost didn't hear them, but Jack's response told me he had.

"Think about this, but don't take too long." He pulled me back to him and kissed me. I closed my eyes, the rest of the world disappeared, and I was transported back to our first kiss. My whole body tingled.

He pulled away and stood, holding my hand and supporting me as I stood slowly per doctor's orders. I made my way inside, Jack right behind me, a hand on the small of my back.

"I need to go shower before we head to Dee's." I spoke as much to Jack as to Shelley, who sat at the table with her laptop.

*** 

Alone in my room, I undressed, then stood beneath the running water in the shower. It felt so incredible, I wished I could stay in this moment forever. When I closed my eyes, the heat of the water relaxed me and helped wash away the dread and fear. Despite the stinging of the water on my wound, I could pretend that the terror in our lives wasn't real. When the heat of the water faded, I turned off the tap, stepped out of the tub, and dried off.

I stood in front of the mirror and couldn't help but stare at my wound. Just as it had been nearly six years ago, it was fresh with stitches holding it closed, persuading it to heal.

I had just finished getting dressed when I heard a quiet knock on the door. I opened it to find Shelley with a quirky smile on her face.

"So, you finally told Jack how you feel."

"How do you know?"

"It's going to take a lot to wipe that grin off his face. You'd think he just got laid for the first time." Shelley made herself comfortable sitting on the end of the bed with one foot tucked up underneath her as usual. "Details, please."

I closed the door, followed Shelley to the bed, and sat down next to her.

"There's not much to tell. I told Jack how I feel. I also told him I don't think I can come back after graduation." I gave Shelley the rundown while I struggled to dry my hair.

Shelley took the towel from me and took over the task. "And ..."

"I told him we'd talk when we get through the week."

"He seems awfully happy just knowing you'll *talk* about being together. What are you holding back?"

"He suggested it might be better to just be together for the time we have instead of holding out for a conversation that might not even be possible when this is all over. I told him I'd think about it."

# Chapter 23

By the time we got back to Shelley's late that afternoon, I was exhausted. The moment we had left the apartment that morning, the hair on the back of my neck had gone up, and the discomfort stuck with me the whole time we were with Deanna and the coven.

Shelley pulled a bottle out of her liquor cupboard and poured herself a drink. "Kevin, you want one?"

"Sure."

"What about the rest of us?" Jack asked.

"You three aren't guests anymore." She waved a finger at Jack, Dave, and I, "So, you'll have to pour your own." A wink supported the hint of sarcasm I'd detected in her voice.

Jack entered the kitchen and grabbed a couple of glasses, holding one up, he gestured toward Dave and me.

"Dave, Liz?"

I saw Dave nod out of the corner of my eye.

"No, thanks, I'm going to go lie down." I stretched and started toward the hall.

He set the glasses on the counter and moved toward the hall to cut me off. "Are you okay?"

I glanced briefly at Shelley. Her back was to me, and she was almost out the door to the balcony.

"I'm fine, really, just tired. It was a long day out there and a lot to take in. I just need to rest."

"Let me know if you need anything." He squeezed my hand.

"I will." He leaned forward and laid a gentle kiss on my forehead before I could turn away and continue to my room. Though I'd expressed my feelings and agreed to his request not to wait to be together, I was apprehensive. I still felt like one of us was going to wind up getting hurt.

Lying on the bed, I closed my eyes and thought about what we had discussed with the coven. One thing stood out from the rest.

*"I'm glad you've decided to be with Jack while time is guaranteed."* Deanna had said as she hugged me goodbye. *When she let go and stood back, her expression hadn't matched her sentiment. She had turned to Maria, and the two had shared a long silent look.*

*"You could be right, my dear."* Maria put a hand on my shoulder and closed her eyes. *"Elizabeth, I fear you may be tainted."*

My mind ran in circles, other bits and pieces of the day churned into blackness.

***

A voice woke me from a dreamless sleep. I sat up, startled, and blinked the sleep from my eyes. I held my breath and listened. All was quiet except for the distant voices of my four roommates, who were still on the balcony.

I closed my eyes and waited for what seemed like an eternity before I heard it again.

I got up and moved slowly toward the voice. I couldn't quite make out the words. They were muffled as if whoever was speaking was covered by blankets or towels or something.

Halfway across the room, I stopped to listen. The voice came again, louder, but still muffled.

I stood, frozen to the spot for a couple of minutes. Then, as if an invisible rope had been tied around my waist, I was pulled toward the voice. I fought to stand my ground but found myself powerless to resist the pull. It eased when I reached the bathroom, and the voice came again. I put my ear against the door so that I could hear better.

"Come in, please. We need to talk." I thought I recognized the voice, but I couldn't quite place it.

I stood, hands at my sides, and watched the door open. Before me stood a young man with sandy-blonde hair and caramel eyes. I recognized him, but I didn't know where from.

"Who are you? What are you doing in my bathroom?"

"I figured this was the best place to get you alone."

"Who are you?" I demanded. I wanted to move toward him, but my feet wouldn't cooperate.

"You're letting your sense of reason betray you, Elizabeth. Don't you remember me?"

Ice replaced the blood in my veins as recognition set in. "That was a drug-induced hallucination. How can you be here?"

"I'm anywhere I want to be, and thanks to you, I will soon be everywhere. Your friends are about to set me free, and when they do, I'm going wipe them and this pathetic town right off the map."

I shook my head. "You can't. You're bound to my property. The witches said so."

"That's what they think. They know a bit, but they don't know enough. You won't defeat me, Elizabeth, but you will set me free. Why do you think I brought you here?"

My heart skipped a beat. "What do you mean you brought me here?" The man's caramel eyes swirled like liquid, and a smile formed on his lips. As attractive as he was, my blood felt cold in his presence.

"Poor Elizabeth, your parents died so tragically, so suddenly." The smile on his face grew as he spoke. A gleam sparkled in his eyes as he pinpointed the moment I understood what he meant.

"It was you? You killed them?" Fire ran through me, my hands clenched. "You *brought* me here." Rage propelled me from my spot. I lifted my arms and stepped toward him. My elbows bent and with another step I shoved as hard as I could. My body followed as I stumbled forward through nothing. I spun and saw the figure waiver and solidify again.

The demon laughed. "A single car with so much damage and absolutely no clues on the road as to what could have caused it. Did you *really* believe that was possible? You must have suspected something otherworldly."

"Why?" I screamed, doubly angered that I had gone right though him and that this thing in front of me had killed my parents just to get my attention.

"Why me?"

"I need you, Elizabeth. I can't get free without you." The thing in front of me lifted an arm to chest level as he nodded his head down and to one side with a sneer on his lips. "Well, I probably could, but it's much more fun to have you to play with. I've always been partial to you, ever since the night you woke me from a five-hundred-year nap." I heard a hint of bitterness as he snapped the p at the end.

*Oh shit, they were right, the witches, it was us who woke the demon. It's all true, and now, Mom, Dad. They're dead because of me … this is all my fault. If I had just stayed away.*

The room started to spin. I closed my eyes and heard the demon laugh. I could feel the room spin faster and faster. As it did, the demon laughed harder and louder until it all stopped at once.

\*\*\*

I opened my eyes to find Jack and Shelley on either side of me. I felt soft carpet beneath my head and upper body, cold tile beneath my legs.

Kevin had his hand on my wrist, probably taking my pulse, and Jack stroked my hair while holding my other hand. I twisted around and saw Deanna and Dave standing a few feet away. Shelley had her phone in hand, appearing to wait for instructions.

I glanced back and forth between Kevin and Jack, then sat up and waited for them to realize I was okay.

As the realization sank in, they let me stand under my own power, although Jack's posture never relaxed, ready to catch me at any moment.

"I'm okay." I tried to reassure them, seeing the concern on their faces.

"What happened?" Shelley asked. "We heard a crash, and when we got here, you were on the floor."

Jack seemed to be having trouble finding his voice.

I shook my head and started out of the bathroom. "Not here. Not in here, please, and I'll take that drink now."

The four followed me out of the bedroom and down the hall. I went straight for the balcony, the guys hot on my heels. Shelley, now confident in my condition, detoured to the kitchen, then joined us on the balcony.

"What the hell, Liz?" Shelley handed me a tumbler half full of bourbon. I took it from her and continued pacing the balcony.

"I woke up and heard a voice. I couldn't tell who it was, so I followed it into the bathroom. It was the demon." Razor blades filled my throat. My eyelids swelled with angry tears before they spilled over and ran down my cheeks. "It planned this whole thing," I forced the words out supressing the scream building in my chest. "And it knows what we're going do and how we're going do it." I shot back the drink Shelley had given me and shivered as it burned its way to my gut then sank into my favourite chair.

Jack stared at me, wearing an expression of disbelief. "What do you mean this was all part of the plan?"

"He told me." I shook my head and corrected myself. "*It* told me. It came to me in human form. The same as the dream I had in the hospital, but I know I wasn't dreaming this time. It brought me back to Evergreen so that we would free it."

"You came here because your parents died." Shelley had her hands on her hips, visibly agitated.

"Shelley, it killed my parents. That was how it got me here. It started *all* of this!"

I watched as understanding spread through them and pinpointed the moment they each needed to sit before their legs gave out.

"Call Dee," I said desperately. "You need a new plan. It knows what we're going to do. I felt like I was being watched all day. It must have been the demon. When we were leaving, Maria said she thought I was tainted. I didn't know what she meant, but I think that's why I was attacked the other day, to strengthen the connection it had from before, so it could spy on us."

I bent forward over my knees, my head in my hands. Tears quickly filled them and dripped through my fingers to the balcony.

"Shelley?" Dave said after a few moments of silence, "why don't you call Dee, you three go meet her somewhere, figure out a new plan? I'll stay here with Liz."

Jack shook his head. "No, Dave, I'll stay. If something happens again, you aren't exactly in a position to help much."

"It obviously doesn't want to kill her. It would have by now if that's what it wanted. Look, man, I know you're worried about her, but I can't move as fast as the rest of you, so it makes sense we have a game plan which doesn't involve me doing a whole lot other than hanging with Liz, and the way I see it, if I'm not part of it, I don't need to know it."

"And I can't know," I added. "Jack, he's right, you know he is. I'll be fine." I emphasized the last words.

Jack regarded each of us in turn. Shelley and Kevin nodded their agreement with Dave. Jack would know he wasn't going to win this argument. It was four to one.

Shelley grabbed the empty glasses and went inside. She closed the patio door behind her. Less than fifteen minutes later, Shelley, Kevin, and Jack were on their way out of the apartment.

\*\*\*

Dave and I sat on the balcony, trying to find a bit of serenity in the last of the sun's rays.

"You know, none of this would have happened if I hadn't come back here."

"That's a moot point, Liz. You *are* here, and it *is* happening. Even if you had known, would you honestly have not come home to put your parents to rest?"

I hung my head.

"No hiding from any of this now."

"Dave, it said it wanted *me*. That it needed me to get out, not any of you, chances are you wouldn't have a broken leg right now if I hadn't shown up."

"Well, you did. Liz, you have to get over this. We don't have time for you to keep blaming yourself for the things that have happened since you arrived in Evergreen. Shit's gonna get real pretty damn quick, and if you don't have your head in the game, we could all be in serious trouble."

"What if I leave town, go somewhere out of reach. I could go to Denver or back to Topeka."

"That might be a good idea, or it might not. It doesn't matter what you do, because if you plan it and anything is planned around any decision you make, the demon could know about it. We don't know how the connection works or how strong it is. Let Dee and her aunts figure this part out and just let go of the guilt. You can't protect everyone, Liz. You need to accept that."

"I know you're right, Dave, but I can't help feeling responsible."

Dave waved his tumbler at me. "I'm gonna need another, and it's way easier for you to get the drinks than it is for me." Dave winked at me and wiggled one of his crutches to emphasize his current disability.

"Okay, what'll it be this time?"

"Same, unless you have a better idea." Dave reached up and handed me his empty glass as I stood to go inside.

I mixed up a round of gin and tonics, then rejoined Dave. We focused on light conversation, keeping well away from what lay ahead. A couple of drinks later, which was not as long as it probably should have been, we got around to the inevitable topic of Jack and me.

"I do love him, Dave, but I don't want to hurt him again."

"That's not really up to you. You love Jack, he loves you. What else matters? If you give it a go and things don't work out, then you break up, and you both know it wasn't meant to be." Dave spoke with a noticeable slur.

I shrugged and took a sip of my drink. I didn't want to think about it, but Dave was all about forcing the issue with me and had been since I got back.

"If you don't try to have a relationship, you will always wonder what could have been. I know he'd go anything for you, do anywhere for you, so if Evergreen is what's stopping you, you have no excuse. And if Evergreen isn't stopping you from being with him, then it's just you." Dave hiccupped.

The gin had made me feel pretty good, so I was surprised when a tear spilled over the edge of my eyelid and ran down my cheek, and as soon as I wiped it way, more followed. I tried in vain to wipe the tears away, but a monsoon had started, and my throat tightened.

"Jesus, Liz, I didn't mean to make you cry."

A laugh hitched its way through the tears, and I threw my hands up, surrendering to the emotion.

"I didn't think I was gonna cry either." I managed to spit the words out between hitches as the torrent continued.

Dave pulled himself up, wobbled on his crutches, and click-stomped his way into the living room to find me a tissue.

As he came back out, I shook my head. Through the tears, it seemed like he was walking normally, and I thought he was Jack.

As he sat beside me, holding out the box of tissue, I realized it was Jack, and the flood started all over again.

"Why are you crying?" Jack's voice was soft and soothing.

"Because I love you, and I'm really mad about it."

"Why would you be mad about it?"

"Because I don't want to hurt you, and I'm scared if we get back together, I will."

"Liz, there's nothing I want more than for us to be together. If it doesn't work out, I'll be okay, because I know at least we tried." He handed me a tissue and let me dry my face, then wrapped me in his arms and kissed my head. "If you let me, I promise I will do everything in my power to keep you safe and happy for as long as it works for us both."

I nestled into his warmth and took a deep breath. I think that was when I made up my mind.

# Chapter 24

I woke up early again the next morning, a semi-truck crashing against the inside of my skull. The light burned my eyes when I made the mistake of opening them, and a thick layer of film coated the inside of my mouth.

I lay with my eyes closed a bit longer, but the pounding wouldn't stop. I knew, no matter how much it hurt, I had to get out of bed to get some Ibuprofen.

*God, how much did we drink last night? I don't even remember getting into bed.*

Before I could open my eyes, I felt a gentle touch move the hair from my face and tuck it behind my ear. Startled, I opened my eyes much wider and faster than I had intended.

"Jack?"

He nodded, love and adoration on his face. I scrutinized him as best I could without moving too much, trying to figure out when he might have come into my room. He was under the blankets, which meant he had probably been here all night.

I sighed and stared him in the eye. "What are you doing in my bed?"

He smiled and rubbed my cheek with his thumb; his hand still lingered around my ear.

"You needed a little help getting into bed last night. Once Shelley got you changed, and we got you into bed, you asked me to stay, so I stayed." He spoke in a near whisper.

Jack must have read the concern on my face, and before I could even ask, he threw back the blankets, revealing his clothes from the night before. "Nothing happened, Liz. I held you until you fell asleep. I figured since you asked me to stay, you might be upset if you woke and I wasn't here."

I closed my eyes again, trying to lessen the impact of the incessant semi in my head.

Jack got up, shaking the bed, then I heard each step he took across the carpet to the bathroom. The door opening was loud enough that I would've sworn it was right beside me. I put the pillow over my head to soften the banging of the pills as Jack spilled a few into his hand.

"That bad, huh?" he whispered when he came back.

"You have no idea. What the hell was I drinking last night?" I sat up slowly, now thankful Jack had slept in my bed last night, so I could avoid moving for the moment.

He handed me a glass of water, and I swallowed the pills he gave me. "The gin was almost gone when we got back, so you and Dave went back to bourbon.

"Oh, God." I put a hand on my head. "What time is it?"

"A little after six."

I groaned. "Can I go back to sleep for a while?"

"Yes, we have a few hours before we need to leave."

Jack moved to leave, but I stretched out a hand to stop him.

"Stay, please. Unless you were planning to get up now, in which case, that's fine."

Jack smiled at me and climbed back in beside me. He stretched out his left arm and waited for me to get comfortable before wrapping himself around me in a protective cocoon. He kissed my head, and I couldn't help but smile to myself as I closed my eyes and waited for the semi to stop slamming into my skull.

When I woke two hours later, the throbbing in my head had all but stopped. I opened my eyes and realized we hadn't moved. Not an inch. Jack still had me wrapped in his arms. I put my hand on his shoulder. I traced the length of his arm with one finger until I heard him murmur.

"How's your head?" he asked in a low whisper.

"Much better. I think I can get up now."

"You're ruining the best dream I've had in years, you know."

"Then stay here and finish your dream. I need to get up. I'm parched and starving."

Jack tightened his grip on me for just a moment before he let me go. I crossed the room and studied him before I closed the bathroom door. My heart sped up, and butterflies danced in my stomach. We'd never actually spent a night next to each other, at least not a whole night.

I turned my attention to the mirror to brush my teeth. The wound, which had been fresh just a few days ago, seemed to be healing much faster than usual. I'd had Kevin remove the stitches, and already, a bright white scar was forming at either end. Most of the stitch marks were barely visible.

A body scrub sat on the counter with a note attached. It was from Dee and her aunts. I read it, then brushed my teeth and got in the shower. I stood still for a moment or two, just letting the water fall over me, my eyes closed, and let my thoughts wander as I often did when I needed to think.

Had I made a mistake asking Jack to stay with me this morning? I had decided to give things a chance, but I hadn't said as much to Jack, at least I don't think I had. Maybe I got so drunk last night because I didn't want to tell him.

I won't tell him just yet. I'll tell him we need to focus on today and stay alive. I will give it serious thought, maybe that will be enough for now.

As I figured out what to say, my body went on autopilot. I found myself rinsing my already washed hair, and then continued by pampering my skin with a good all over exfoliation with the scrub sent home with Shelley and Jack. The note had said it had protective properties that would be useful tonight.

I applied the scrub from head to toe and worked it into my skin as best I could, then waited a few minutes before rinsing well as instructed. I felt renewed as I got out of the shower.

\*\*\*

Jack was gone when I emerged from the bathroom, so I dressed quickly and went to the kitchen to get coffee. I found Jack on the balcony with Dave, Kevin, and Shelley. They were deep in conversation and didn't seem to hear me open the slider.

I stepped into the warm morning air. The four continued their conversation even when I stood right next to them. I cleared my throat to alert them to my presence.

"Good morning, you guys."

Shelley's back was to me. She jumped when I spoke. Dave's arm jerked; coffee flew from his cup. Jack leaped from his chair to avoid the coffee. Kevin clapped a hand to his chest. The four of them stared at me.

"Jesus Christ, Liz. You really thought it would be funny to sneak up on me? After all, that's happened?"

"How did you not hear me? I'm wearing flip flops for Christ's sake, and I wasn't sneaking." The words rang harshly in my ears.

Jack and the brothers stared at me, wide-eyed.

"How long have you been standing there?" Dave set his empty cup down on the table beside him. His shirt was soaked.

"You didn't make a sound walking over here, and I didn't see you coming either."

"Okay, that's just weird. I could maybe understand Shelley, but not the four of you. I'm not that quiet, not even barefoot." I gawked at Jack and Kevin. "And you two should have seen me coming."

Shelley stood and faced me; her expression changed from shock to awe. She examined me from head to toe and nodded.

"Your hair's wet, so you had a shower already. Did you use the scrub Dee sent over?"

"Yes, why?"

"She said it had protective properties, that it would shield you. I assumed it would just shield you from the demon, but I wonder if she meant it would shield you from everyone."

"That has to be it." Jack came over to me and wrapped one arm around my back and kissed my cheek then continued into the kitchen.

"Sorry about freaking out on you." Shelley sat back down, and I took the seat next to her.

"So, you guys really didn't know I was there?"

Kevin picked up his coffee to take another sip. "Nope, not until you spoke. I guess we'll have to let the others know."

"Yeah, don't want anyone getting injured because they don't know you're standing next to them," Dave said.

"I hope the effects last that long," I said. "Maybe I should have waited until later to use it."

"Maybe we should call Dee, find out what else to expect," Kevin said.

Jack hurried back from the kitchen with supplies to clean up the coffee and a clean shirt for Dave.

"Thanks, man."

"No problem. I know you hate sitting in wet clothes."

"Is there anyone who doesn't?" Dave changed shirts and set the wet one on the table beside him.

"Liz, how come you get to look so good this morning?" Shelley asked. "The state you were in last night, you should be hanging hard right about now."

"Pills and sleep." I took a sip of my coffee. "Mmm, and I think demon energy might have something to do with it, too."

"What?" All four of them gaped at me, their expressions demanding an explanation.

I had layered on my clothing as I thought it might still be a bit cool out, so I removed my hoodie and pointed at my wound.

"This amount of healing is unnatural. Maria said she thought I was tainted. And we know the demon brought me back to Evergreen, so I figure it's been healing me. Maybe its energy cures hangovers, too."

Dave's face scrunched in thought as he processed my statement. "Makes sense, I guess. Wanna share some of that healing power over here." He pointed at his broken leg, then peeked into his cup and drank the last of his coffee.

Jack and Dave both got up from their chairs and went inside. Shelley took the opportunity to grill me.

"So, what was that all about, with Jack? The hug, the kiss on the cheek?"

"I woke up this morning, and he was in my bed. I asked him to stay while I slept my headache away."

"So, are you guys back together now, or what?"

I smiled. "I haven't told Jack as much yet, but I decided he and everyone else is right. There may not be a future to worry about, so why wait."

216

\*\*\*

No one would tell me about the new plan, even though I was shielded from them. Deanna's aunts weren't sure how far the shield went. All I knew was that things were going down tonight, before the demon had a chance to get any stronger.

The six of us decided to go to the diner for breakfast for old time's sake. We tried to keep the conversation light, but none of us wanted to go into this fight with things unsaid. As a result, we went from laughter to sincerity, and a few tears were shed. I apologized for the way I had left and promised no matter what I decided to do after I finished school, that I would keep in touch with all of them, not just Shelley.

Walking back from the diner, Jack and I lagged behind the others. I had one more thing to say.

"I've made a decision, Jack." I stared at the sidewalk. The cracks resembled spiderwebs that had been torn up by insects.

"You have my attention."

"You were right about not waiting for a future that may or may not exist. I want to be with you, now, in the time we're guaranteed. If we get a future, we'll make decisions about it together."

I reached for his hand and squeezed, then gazed at him as we continued our stroll back to Shelley's.

"I'm so glad you said that." He pulled me to his side, raised our joined hands up and over my head so our arms wrapped around my waist.

"Hey, guys, we'll catch up to you in a bit," Jack said. "We're gonna take a walk." He tilted his head toward the park. "Come on."

A light breeze swept the willow branches and wafted the scent of late summer flowers into the air around us. We strolled toward the far side of the park where a stream cut through. Benches dotted the bank. We picked one that was off on its own and sat down. The water rippled over rocks in the streambed and lapped against earth walls.

"I'm being selfish." Jack twirled a small section of my hair in his fingers. "But I needed to have you to myself for a while. I hope you don't mind."

"Not at all." I was lost in the depths of his blue eyes. I allowed the feelings I had suppressed for years to take over. Memories flooded my mind and morphed into visions of a future I longed for.

We sat in silence, taking each other in, fingers roaming, memorizing features, and the feel of one another's skin. I couldn't speak, afraid of spoiling what little time we may have together.

Jack's phone buzzed.

"Don't look."

"I have to." He pulled his phone from his pocket and read the text aloud.

TIME'S UP.

We faced each other, neither ready to leave. Jack put his hand to my cheek, and I leaned into his touch and closed my eyes. His lips were on mine. I tasted the salt of tears in our kiss. He pulled back and dried my cheek with his thumb. I opened my tear-filled eyes. He took my hand in his and led me away from our tiny piece of heaven.

# Chapter 25

"So, you still aren't going to fill me in on the plan?" I asked Deanna over the phone.

"No. The shield of protection we gave you seems to be working, although we're not sure whether it's you or the demon that is shielded from us. It's safer if you don't know the details. We'll tell you what you need to know when you need to know it, okay? For now, just be at your house at seven. You will have things to do, trust me."

"I do trust you. I just really hate being kept in the dark."

"I know. I'm sorry. I'll see you soon." Deanna hung up, and I locked my phone and stuck it in my back pocket.

Deanna had given me a small list of supplies to gather, so I was about to leave my room when I sensed movement behind me. I spun around to find Jack in the open doorway. He knocked as I faced him.

"Hey," I said, my voice squeaking.

"How are you holding up?" He crossed the room and stood close enough to grasp my hand between his. "Can I do anything for you?"

"No, I'm okay. I mean, I'm scared and nervous, but I'm pretty sure that's how we're all feeling. Tonight is literally do or die."

"Yeah, I know. I'm about to head out with Kevin and Shelley, but I wanted to tell you I love you."

"I love you, too."

He hugged me for a moment, then let me go just enough to take my face in his hands and kiss me. It felt like this was the last kiss we'd ever have, everything he wanted to say, everything he felt was on his lips, and the whole world melted away for the moment.

Before he released his hold on me, he stared into my eyes as if trying to find all the answers he was looking for.

"Be careful tonight."

My voice was lost to me. I nodded when he stepped back. He left me standing there. I hoped it wouldn't be the last I saw of him.

Shelley came in a moment later and handed me an envelope. "This is from Dee. Don't read it until she texts you. It's your instructions. I'll see you at the house tonight." Shelley turned to walk away.

"Shelley, wait." She turned back toward me. "Look, I just want you to know ..." I couldn't finish. Shelley and I had never been too sentimental with each other.

"Don't you dare start crying, Liz. We got through this before, and we'll get through it again. We have help, this time, so just don't!"

"I know, but last time I wasn't connected to it, I was out there with you guys, and we still lost Stacey."

Shelley closed the gap between us.

"We didn't have the coven last time, and we're all older and presumably smarter now. You, of all people, need to think positive and stay strong, Liz. If you let the demon get into your head, that could be it for all of us."

"You're right. I know. I just, just don't die, okay." I threw my arms around her and squeezed for all I was worth.

"If you don't kill me now, I'll do my best to stay alive tonight." She spoke in a high pitch, as though I were squeezing the air out of her.

A small, nervous laugh escaped each of us, and I released Shelley from my grip. We each raised a hand, connecting our fingers and thumbs in the shape of a heart. It had been our thing when 'I love you' was the only thing left, and we couldn't face the words.

She left, and I waited in my room until I heard the apartment door close.

\*\*\*

I grabbed my backpack and went to gather the items on my list. I started in the kitchen, looking through Shelley's cupboards and the pantry, but couldn't find what I needed.

"Hey, Dave, we're going to need to stop at the store on the way out to the house. I can't find any of the stuff on this list from Dee. We should leave now, so we're not late."

I heard the metallic click of Dave's crutches as he came down the hall. He had a bag of his own slung over one shoulder, resting against his back.

We settled into small talk, an effort to shift our minds from what was coming and ease our fear. We chatted all the way to the grocery store.

Dave hobbled along as I perused the aisles to find the items on my list.

"Coarse salt, white and purple candles, wooden matches, incense, and lavender oil. I guess that does it." I checked off the list.

"What's this stuff for?"

"I'm not sure, but I have to assume Dee knows what she's doing."

Stocked with supplies, we got in my car and drove out to the property I had abandoned over a week ago.

\*\*\*

As we pulled into the driveway, tension dropped over us like a net. I stopped just a few feet into the driveway, apprehension taking over for a moment.

"It's okay, Liz. You're not doing this alone. I'll be here with you all night. I know I'm not one-hundred percent able-bodied, but we'll get the job done."

I regarded Dave and inhaled deeply, then let my breath out.

"I know, you're right." I found the accelerator and drove the rest of the way up to the house. I pulled the car around, ready for a quick getaway for all the good it would do. We were about to fight a demon, not preparing for an earthquake or fire.

We got out of the car, and I grabbed the bag of supplies while Dave slung his duffel bag across his body. He hopped up the stairs to the porch, both crutches in one hand.

No one else had arrived yet, so we sat on the couch under the living room window and waited to find out what was next. It would have been a beautiful evening, if not for our impending battle with a demon. The only noise was the rustling of a slight breeze through the trees. I considered the evening sky where only a few small clouds lingered. Light would begin to fade soon, and once it was dark, there would be no turning back.

Less than five minutes later, my phone buzzed. I pulled it from my pocket and read the text from Deanna.

*Go into the kitchen. Set up the candles and pour a salt circle. It should look like the picture I'm sending. Text me when you're done.*

"Okay, Dave, we're on."

I got up and led the way inside and down the hall to the kitchen. I set the bag of supplies on the island and opened the picture Dee had sent.

The candles were arranged in a pentagram. White and purple sat at opposing ends of each arm, and salt ran between them. In the center was a glass of water, the incense placed behind it, and positioned so that it was at the head of the pentagram. Around the entire set up was a circle of salt about a foot out from the points of the pentagram.

I moved the nook table to allow enough space, then set to work. It took about fifteen minutes to set it all up and finish pouring the salt circle. Neither Dave nor I said a single word the entire time.

I texted Deanna.

*Done. What's next?*

My phone buzzed within seconds. Dee must have had her next instruction waiting to send.

*Sprinkle the whole area with the lavender oil. Light the candles and the incense, then recite the words on the paper in the envelope Shelley gave you. We'll be there in about 20 minutes.*

I followed Deanna's instructions, then opened the envelope and pulled out a small piece of paper that smelled of lilac. I drew in a long breath to steady myself. I nodded at Dave to signal I was about to start.

"Return to the ether. Be gone, I say. I protect my home from negative entities. This will be. And so, it is. And it harms no one. It will be done."

I followed the instructions and walked in a clockwise path inside the salt, and then followed each of the lines of the pentagram, finally walking another clockwise circle inside the salt. Then I stopped, faced the center of the pentagram, and bent down, extinguishing each of the candles in turn, beginning with the last one I had lit. When all the candles were out, I stepped backward out of the salt circle, careful to keep it intact.

I joined Dave on the far side of the island.

"Dee's note says that was supposed to remove any non-physical entities. Let's hope it worked." I checked my phone and noted the time since Dee's last text. "They should be here any minute."

As if on cue, two vehicles came up the driveway and continued past the house to the north field. About a hundred feet from the tree line, they stopped at an angle that shielded the occupants from view as they got out.

"I guess that's part of making sure you don't have any more information than necessary," Dave said.

"I guess so."

I pulled out my phone and was about to send Dee a text when there was a knock at the living room door. Dave and I both jumped at the unexpected sound. I clapped a hand over my heart. "Jesus!" I rolled my eyes and glanced at Dave.

He shrugged. "Go answer it, I guess."

I hurried down the hall, Dave close behind, crutches clicking all the way. In the living room, I peered through the curtain before opening the door.

"God, Dee, you scared the crap out of us. Come on in."

"Hey, Liz. I can't sense you at all. I guess that means the shield is still working, but I don't like not knowing whether you're still tied to the demon or not."

Deanna handed me another envelope. "I'm not staying, I just came to check on you and give you this. You can read it, silently, to practice. I'll text you when it's time to read it out loud. Good luck, and stay safe, you two."

Deanna hugged us both, then took off out to the field to join the others.

# Chapter 26

The sun set over the trees and colored the sky a deep, reddish orange. The light streamed through the kitchen window and bathed the room in red and late summer heat. A chill ran down my spine. I hoped this was not an omen as the coven would start their ritual soon.

Dave and I went out to the porch and watched the sun slip below the tree line.

Daylight faded. In just moments, a new battle would begin, one which would either change my life or end it.

Our unease reached into the air between us like lightning bolts in reverse.

Dave tapped his good foot on the boards.

Butterflies boiled in my stomach, and my heart raced.

We stood silent for several minutes as the sky darkened.

"Liz, have you noticed there are no bugs out tonight?"

"I hadn't, but you're right." The hair on the back of my neck stood on end—the nocturnal sounds I was used to were missing, signs that didn't bode well. Evil was here, and the animals could feel it. "I think we better go inside, Dave. I feel exposed out here."

"Yeah, me too."

I checked my phone as we entered the kitchen. It was just after eight. I stood at the sink and peered out the window. I saw an orange glow of flames leap into the air and knew they had begun.

"No turning back now," I said. "Fire's burning."

\*\*\*

I felt like a child waiting for punishment. Anxiety radiated out of Dave like electricity while we watched the flicker of distant flames from the kitchen table. The tension between and around us was palpable.

"I wish I knew what was going on out there. I feel useless, just sitting here."

"Me too." Dave tapped his cast with his crutch.

I moved to the window and watched as if it had become a view screen. All I could see was the flicker of orange from their Fire of Protection, and it did nothing to calm my nerves. I paced between the window and the porch, skirting the salt circle and pentagram on the floor.

Without warning, a deep throbbing started at the center of my wound. I rotated my arm, and the searing pain I had come to know as a sign of transformation ripped through me. This time the change was not limited to my wound.

A flash of white obscured my vision. When it cleared, I was standing in the forest. The coven's fire of protection burned bright in front of me. I could see

Shelley and Jack trying to fight off strange looking creatures. I moved closer and realized I couldn't hear anything.

There was no crackle or heat from the flames. I heard no voices, though I saw mouths moving. I blinked and rubbed my eyes. I was back in the kitchen with Dave.

"That was ... odd," I said. "This connection with the demon—I think I can see what it sees."

"What do you mean?"

"I saw them out there, just now. I saw Shelley and Jack and the fire, but there was no sound, no heat from the flames."

"You need to figure out how to do that again. Maybe you just found a way to get into the fight." A small, hopeful smile pulled up the corners of Dave's mouth. He might just be on to something.

Half a dozen unsuccessful attempts and twenty minutes later, I was still in the kitchen with Dave. He had been watching with bated breath, so as not to break my concentration.

"This sucks. You did it once. There has to be a way to do it again. Try doing exactly what you did the first time."

"I have. Six times. The only difference ..."

"What?"

"My wound. It was throbbing, and I rotated my arm like this." I repeated the movement. As we both had hoped, the searing pain ripped through me. A flash of white followed. This time, red pinpoints skittered through the white.

\*\*\*

I heard chanting over the crackle of the witches' smokeless fire. I could smell the dirt and leaf litter on the forest floor. I took a few steps, dried pine needles crunched. I looked down. These feet were not my own; they were talons. Somehow, I had done it, I had gotten into the demon's head and was seeing, hearing, and feeling what it felt.

The demon moved toward the fire and my friends, but they didn't see it.

Shelley stood about fifty feet to Jack's left. Both had their backs to the fire, facing the tree line.

"I don't like this," she shouted. "It's too quiet all of a sudden."

"I know," Jack replied and checked his phone. "They've been at this for almost an hour already. I expected more of a fight."

Roughly fifty feet to his right, Kevin stood, facing north. "Come on, Jack, don't jinx it. Stay focused. No telling what we're going to get."

As if Jack's statement had been a summoning, unnatural screams from all around the circle met Kevin's words.

Out of nowhere, a creature appeared in front of Kevin. It was nothing I'd seen before. It resembled a raccoon but had the tail of a scorpion and moved on talons.

I felt the demon's mouth curl up, no doubt smiling at the beasts it brought forth.

Kevin made contact, and one of the creatures flew back and fell to the ground. To my surprise, it vanished in a cloud of dust.

The demon conjured another creature, this one bigger than the last, and sent it after Deanna. It scrambled toward her on a dozen feet, its millipede-like body raised like a cobra ready to strike. As it gained striking distance, it snapped its pinchers. Deanna turned her head and raised crossed arms in defense. The monster exploded in front of her. "How the hell?" She asked when she opened her eyes.

Around the circle of fire, each of my friends contended with demonic creatures.

The demon smiled as it watched my friends struggling to defeat creature after creature. Each time my friends were successful, bigger and stronger monstrosities sprang forth.

A choked scream from Shelley caught my ear. The demon laughed and continued his onslaught, still unseen.

It watched as Kevin twirled the sharp side of an ax outward and took a final swing at the creature that leaped toward him. The blade made contact, splitting the thing in two. A tar-like substance oozed from the monster and glistened in the firelight.

"Dee, give my spot some cover, I'm going to check on Shelley." Kevin ran along the wall of fire and found Shelley on the ground, struggling to fend off three dog sized creatures. One bit into her shoulder. She howled. The other two took turns nipping at her feet. She kicked, managed to make contact, and sent one of the attackers flying.

The demon rubbed its gnarled hands together with glee. Kevin turned his ax sideways, blade up to avoid further injury to Shelley, and stepped into a golf swing.

Shelley screamed as the creature's head snapped to the side, a chunk of her flesh in its mouth. It spat out the flesh and shook its head. It scraped its clawed feet in the dirt, then charged. Kevin was ready, the weapon high over his head. He brought it down hard and fast as the thing readied itself to jump. A guttural scream came from the monster when the ax-head made contact and stopped it, dead.

The other two creatures sneered at each other as if communicating strategy. They lunged simultaneously at Kevin; dagger-sharp teeth bared. He sidestepped, and they missed him, one hit the wall of fire and fell to the ground in flames. The other creature scrambled back to its feet. Claws skittered in the dirt as it tried to gain traction. Kevin turned and swung. He hit the beast with the blunt side of the ax, sending it back a few feet. The crunch of bones cracking filled the air.

The creature stood and grunted several times as if trying to catch its breath.

Kevin glanced over at Shelley. She was still on the ground, screaming. The creature seemed to notice this split-second lapse in Kevin's attention. It recoiled, bent its back legs, then sprang and latched onto Kevin's arm. The attack sent Kevin backward several steps. He shook his arm, but the creature held on. He grabbed at it with his opposite hand and managed to pry it loose. Then he flung the creature into the air as high as he could, swinging at it when it fell back toward him. The ax sliced through the creature. It dropped, hitting the ground with a thud. Black tar poured from the two halves of the body.

The demon watched as Kevin dropped to Shelley's side to assess her. She was bleeding badly, and so was Kevin. The demon took pleasure in this.

Through the demon's eyes, I watched as Kevin pulled off his shirt. He tore a strip from the bottom and tied it tight around his wound, then balled the rest of the shirt, and applied it to Shelley's shoulder. He ripped his belt from his waist and cinched it around Shelley's arm to hold the makeshift bandage in place.

My phone buzzed. I was transported back to my body in the kitchen. The change had me dizzy for a moment, and my phone buzzed again.

"Dave, we need to go," I said without even looking at my phone.

"What did you see?" I could hear the concern in his voice.

"Shelley and Kevin. She's hurt bad. And Kevin needs a bandage for his arm." I had already found the first aid kit my parents kept in the kitchen.

"Come on. You need to come, too. You'll have to get Shelley back here somehow, and I'm going to have to stay out there to replace her." I helped Dave stand, then led the way out to my car and sped out to help our friends.

# Chapter 27

"Dave, wait here." I slammed the car into park and leaped out without killing the ignition. I bolted the short distance to Kevin and Shelley.

"Liz, help me get her back to the car," Kevin said.

We picked Shelley up as carefully as we could. Dave opened the back door, and we sat Shelley on the edge of the seat. I held her while Kevin climbed in behind her from the other side.

"Shelley, are you hurt anywhere else?" Kevin eased her into a prone position so he could assess her better.

"I don't t-t-think so." She panted between convulsions. She'd blanched as shock had set in.

"Shelley, look at me, you need to slow your breathing. That thing took a pretty decent chunk out of your shoulder, and you're going into shock. You're going to be okay, but we need to get your breathing under control."

I handed him the blanket from my trunk, and he draped it over her.

Shelley turned to Kevin and nodded. He took a deep breath in through his nose and let it out slowly. Shelley did her best to copy him. They did this a few times until her breathing returned to normal.

"Okay, you good?" Not waiting for an answer from Shelley, Kevin glanced at me. "You need to go take over for her. Dave can help me here. We can't let anything get through that fire. The witches are inside. We need to protect them."

I ran to Shelley's spot and found the ax on the ground. I bent to pick it up, and something swooped past my head. I searched for it but couldn't see much in the dim firelight.

A twig snapped behind me. I spun around and almost lost my balance. I straightened and found myself face to face with the demon in human form.

I was both transfixed and repulsed. The glow from the witch's fire reacted with his essence, and the man-form wavered. For an instant, I saw the true shape of the demon. Its skin appeared red and scaled, sharp bones protruded at every joint.

*Shit, I'm in trouble.*

I tried to call out, but my voice escaped me.

A gust of wind fanned the flames of the fire, and the demon's human form retook shape.

"There you are, Elizabeth. Kind of you to join me tonight. Together, we are going to destroy that annoying coven and your friends along with them. I've waited a long time for this."

I shook my head in protest. I opened my mouth, my voice back in my command.

"I won't let you." I wasn't about to wait for Deanna's instruction. I heard the chanting from within the circle of fire. I figured, by their tempo and volume, the sisters must be nearing completion.

"You don't have a choice in this. They will be defeated. I am going to start with your friends, and then the witches will be defenseless. I think I'll save your boyfriend for last. And then, Elizabeth, you will be mine." The demon's human form grinned and stepped toward me.

I removed the small sheet of paper from my pocket and read it out loud, trying not to trip over the unfamiliar words.

The demon took another step toward me. He raised a hand, and I was shoved backward and fell hard on my ass. I scrambled back to my feet and continued to read.

"Uh, uh, uh. I don't think so." The demon shifted and again raised his hand toward me, this time with more force. I released my grip on the ax and was flung into the air. My arms and legs flailed as I tried to stay upright. I slammed into a tree and felt my back crack. Nausea rose into my throat. I barely had a chance to breathe before I hit the ground, and the impact winded me again. I landed on my side. Something crunched beneath me. Pain surged through my body. I resisted the urge to throw up as the sensation passed through my gut. I lay on the ground for a moment, waiting for my senses to return before trying to push myself up.

Agony burned up my arm like fire. A cry escaped my lips. The demon laughed as it sauntered toward me.

I screamed as the demon-man bent down and grabbed me with one hand. It straightened, lifting me several feet in the air then set me on my feet. It locked eyes with me and held my gaze as it shrunk to human size.

As much as I wanted to, I couldn't turn away. The liquid caramel eyes had me gripped in their stare. The demon leaned in closer, hypnotizing me. In human form, it closed the small space between us and laid its mouth on mine.

My mind swam under the demon's spell. It broke the kiss, tilted its head skyward, and laughed, the sound maniacal and triumphant.

"You're mine, and I'm free!" it bellowed into the night, the man-form wavered, and the beast inside grew.

The demon turned toward the circle of fire surrounding the coven and took a deep breath. As it prepared to exhale, the flames rose several feet and formed a dome over the coven.

"Liz. Now! Read the incantation." I knew Deanna was yelling, but her voice was distant, I had no idea where she was. I blinked, but the action seemed to take much longer than usual. Seconds later, Deanna and Jack ran into the clearing in slow motion.

The demon raised a hand and flung the two of them backward.

The world went quiet. I stood stuck as if in hardening molasses, my motion slowed to a sloth's pace.

I helplessly watched while the demon strode toward my fallen friends in its pure form. This time it didn't waver. It bent and picked up both Jack and Deanna by their waists. He stalked back toward me, one under each arm.

The demon dropped them about five feet from me. I heard their breath rush out of their lungs when they impacted the ground.

Glued to my spot, I stood unblinking as the demon picked up Jack by one leg.

Deanna struggled to her feet. She staggered sideways, glanced at the ground, then steadied herself. She stared at me and spoke.

"Liz. What. Are. You. Waiting. For? Read. The. Incantation." Deanna's words floated through the air, landing on my ears one by one. I didn't understand what they meant.

"You. Need. To. Read. It. Now. It's. Our. Last. Chance." Deanna's lips moved out of sync with this new batch of words. I dragged my eyes shut, then opened them at the same slow pace. I felt as though I was floating, lost in a dream space with nothing to anchor me.

The demon reappeared in my field of vision with Jack in tow. It dragged him alongside Deanna then dropped his foot. It stared at me with caramel eyes. Without releasing my gaze, it waved a hand. Jack howled in pain. The demon studied my reaction. Nothing.

From the corner of my eye, I saw it flick the other wrist. Deanna screamed. I couldn't even twitch.

"Liz, please." Jack's voice. "It's killing us. You need to read the paper."

His voice was thin and distant.

I was swimming in warm liquid caramel, and it felt good.

The demon picked up Jack and held him between us, so I would be sure to see him. I blinked.

"I wonder how far I can take this without you even trying to intervene," the demon said.

Deanna lay behind him, writhing in pain. I had no idea what it had done to them or how badly they might be hurt.

The demon swung Jack back and forth in front of me like a pendulum. My gaze followed left to right as the demon continued to swing Jack. My gaze and my body became one. I sank to the ground and lay on my side.

The demon, with an air of satisfaction, dropped Jack from the crest of his swing. I saw every second as it occurred.

The demon's clawed fingers uncurled.

Free of its grip, Jack fell in slow motion. He landed with his back to me. The thud followed, then I heard his breath escape in a huff.

I blinked. Something inside me tingled.

Red seeped from beneath Jack's tousled hair.

Something in me snapped.

My senses returned. Butterflies erupted in my stomach as I realized the situation. Jack lay in a heap in front of me, Deanna writhed in pain behind him.

I felt the slip of paper still clenched in my hand. I closed my eyes and recited the words from memory. I whispered at first, barely loud enough for myself to hear. I found my feet as I continued. I uttered the words as fast as I could and increased my volume the closer I got to where I had left off. I kept going this time, my eyes still closed. I spoke with speed and purpose.

I opened my eyes. The demon stopped in its tracks and bent to face me at eye-level.

"I said, no!" its voice boomed.

I got to my feet.

It raised a hand, and I stumbled backward.

I continued to recite.

The demon appeared to shrink.

The coven's chanting synchronized with mine.

The demon wavered. It waved again. This time there was no effect.

The witches reached a feverish pace, their voices seemed to echo off the hills behind us.

The demon stalked toward me, but I stood my ground and shouted into the night. I reached a crescendo in time with the coven. A thunderous boom erupted, and the fire dome went out. Blue light emanated from their midst.

We yelled the final word of the incantation. The blue light exploded out from the center of the coven and engulfed the demon.

I heard another explosion, and the blue light rushed into the demon and disappeared, the demon with it.

*It's over.*

I sank to my knees and grabbed my arm. I pulled it close to my body as a fresh wave of pain coursed through me. I saw Jack and Deanna on the ground. My body went numb, the world tilted sideways, and darkness took over.

# Chapter 28

I woke up in the hospital for the second time in less than two weeks. Jack was a familiar sight in a chair next to my bed. The electronic beeping of the machines seemed to be our new song.

"Hey," I said gruffly.

"Hi," Jack stood and picked up my hand.

"Here again? What now?" My voice cracked.

Jack handed me a cup of water. "Here, it sounds like your throat is pretty sore, but not too much, okay?"

I nodded and took several tiny sips then handed the cup back to Jack.

"You broke your arm and needed surgery to fix it." Jack put the cup on the table beside him.

"What about Shelley? She was hurt pretty bad."

Jack kissed my forehead.

"You need to rest. I'll tell you everything later."

I closed my eyes and let myself drift back into the darkness provided by the morphine drip.

\*\*\*

"She woke up for a few minutes," Jack whispered to someone. "That was a couple of hours ago."

"Dr. Roberts," a female voice interrupted. I heard shuffling footsteps, and the new voice moved away.

"Excuse me, Jack. I need to check on another patient. I'll be back to check on Liz in a few minutes." The doctor's voice belonged to a woman, too. I waited until I was sure they were out of the room.

I heard a chair move and turned my head toward the sound before I opened my eyes. Jack smiled. I couldn't help but smile back. He grasped my hand and rubbed his thumb over the back of it.

"Was that the doctor?"

"Yeah, the surgeon who fixed your arm. I think she must be checking on all her patients before she goes home."

"Goes home?"

Jack nodded. "It's after six. Who knows how long she's been here?"

"I am so tired of losing time. I sure hope that's going to stop now."

"Well, you've had good reason to be losing time lately. It's over. We did it."

"So, it worked then? That wasn't just my imagination?"

"No. I talked to Dee this afternoon. She said Maria and the sisters stayed at your place to make sure, and none of them sensed the demon's energy anymore."

I breathed a sigh of relief. "Have you slept at all? You look exhausted."

"I had a short nap while you were sleeping. Don't worry about me, just concentrate on getting better so you can get out of here." He squeezed my hand as he spoke.

A woman in a white coat entered the room and approached my bed.

"That's good advice. You should listen to him." The woman smiled and nodded toward Jack.

He stood and moved to the other side of the bed, giving the doctor the space she'd need. She paused at the foot of my bed to grab my chart.

"I'm Dr. Roberts, an orthopedic surgeon. I just wanted to check on you before I go home." She grabbed my hand and ran her pen over my palm.

"I'm just making sure you still have good sensation and blood flow to your hand. You had a severe break, and sometimes there's nerve damage. You don't seem to be having any issue with that, however. I'm happy so far, but we're going to keep you overnight. I'm sure you're aware there can be unexpected complications with any surgery."

"Yes." I was sure she was aware of my recent hospital stay.

"Okay, Elizabeth. Get some rest and listen to your boyfriend. Concentrate on healing, it's hard work. I'll see you in the morning."

\*\*\*

Jack stayed with me all night again, leaving only to get something to eat. The next morning the doctor signed my release.

Jack hadn't said a word since the wheelchair had arrived in my room. I got nervous as we entered the underground parking lot.

"Why are you so quiet?"

"Shelley's wounds were a lot worse than Kevin thought."

"What do you mean."

We reached his truck, and Jack set the brake on the chair so I could stand. He stepped ahead, opened my door, and helped me in.

"I'll be right back."

He made sure I was comfortable before closing the door. I didn't recall him being the evasive type. My stomach tied itself in knots, and horrible images inserted themselves into my head while I waited for him to come back. I watched him the whole way back to the door where he left the chair then trudged back, his head down the entire way.

Once he was seated in the truck, I asked again.

"What do you mean, Shelley's wounds were worse than Kevin thought? If she's here, why didn't we go see her?"

He twisted in his seat, enough to look me in the eye when he took my hand. He dropped his gaze and rubbed the back of my hand with his thumbs.

"Jack." My voice cracked, fear overtaking annoyance.

"She didn't make it, Liz." The words came out strangled. He hadn't been stalling. He just wasn't able to speak.

I saw his tears before I realized my own were falling. I leaned in toward him and let him pull me across the bench seat. We sat with his arms awkwardly around me, both of us heaving with full-body sobs.

I don't know how long we sat like that before he straightened up.

He brushed the matted hair away from my face and did his best to dry my cheek with his hand. "I'm so sorry, Liz. They worked so hard to save her, but she'd lost too much blood."

"How long?" I choked out the only words I could.

"She was gone before the sun came up." He stared out the windshield and wiped his tear-soaked face, then glanced at me. "We should go. The others will be waiting."

I nodded, unable to speak, tears still flowing silently, soaking my shirt. I hugged myself with my good arm. Jack put the truck in gear and left the parking lot. I was thankful for the thick, gray clouds that had filled the sky. Sun and warmth would have felt disrespectful today. As soon as we were on the road, Jack draped his arm around me and pulled me tight to him. I leaned my head into his shoulder and closed my eyes. A lifetime of memories and five years of regret tumbled over in my mind. My best friend was gone. My soul writhed with pain, and I almost wondered if this was even close to what Deanna had felt when we lost Stacey, but my brain wouldn't complete a single thought before it grabbed at the next one. Thankfully, there was Jack.

\*\*\*

We parked outside Shelley's building. It felt wrong somehow, but Jack still didn't have a place to live, so it made sense. He waited until I was ready, then helped me out of the truck and into the building. We rode the elevator to the penthouse in silence as Shelley and I had done my first night in town.

Dave, Kevin, and Deanna were seated in the living room, waiting for us as Jack had said. The furniture had been put back to its original arrangement, and the extra mattress was gone. It took me a minute to realize it wasn't because of Shelley, but because the demon was gone. Guarding each other was no longer a necessity.

After a lengthy group hug, they let me sit.

"You look cold, Liz. I'll get you a blanket." Jack left a kiss on my forehead, then started down the hall.

"How's your arm?" Deanna sat in the chair next to the sofa.

I stared at the sling I had forgotten about and shrugged. "Sore, but it'll heal. Are you all okay? Jack hasn't said much." I felt tears moisten the corners of my eyes.

"I'm a little bruised, but for the most part, I'm okay." Deanna reached for a cup that sat on the coffee table.

Dave pointed to his casted leg. "I guess I should be thankful. This thing kept me out of harm's way."

"I'm all right, too," Kevin said. "Better shape than Jack and Dee, that's for sure." Kevin pulled a chair over from the table to sit on.

Jack returned with a blanket. He draped it around my shoulders, then sat down beside me.

"What happened last night?" I asked. "I'm not sure how much I remember."

"It all seemed too easy to begin with," Kevin said. "Just these strange creatures that looked like a bunch of different animals mixed together. They were nasty, but not difficult to kill."

"Yeah, a good headshot seemed to do the trick," Jack added.

"I kind of saw that." I explained how I had been inside the demon's head, seeing what it saw. "I knew Shelley had been hurt before I got the text. I saw it happen. But once we got out there, something else happened. Dee, I thought for sure that thing was going to kill you. How did you stop it?"

"I'm not sure. I talked to Maria about it when they were cleaning up, and they think I somehow channeled Stacey's telekinesis. She said there are stories of witches who can siphon power from other living witches, but Maria has never heard of anyone channeling the gift of a dead witch before. The whole coven is researching what it might mean." She set her cup on the table. "I wanted to ask you something, Liz. You seemed like you were almost happy to watch the demon attacking Jack and me. What was that all about?"

"It was strange. The two of you were on the other side of the circle. When I first got out there, when I went to cover Shelley's spot, it came to me in human form again." I eyed Jack, hesitant, then spoke to Deanna. "It, it kissed me. Put me in some kind of trance, I think. When you two showed up, it was all slow motion. I saw what was going on, but I couldn't react. It was like a dream." I returned my attention to Jack. "Right up until I saw you bleeding. When I recognized you were seriously injured, the trance broke. I recited the incantation, and the demon disappeared in a burst of blue light. That's the last thing I remember."

Jack rubbed the back of his head. "The blood you saw was from a tiny cut on the back of my head. It didn't even need stitches." He turned around so I could see for myself.

We talked for a while longer, but we were all tired and needed rest. When Dee and the guys left, Jack went to get us some dinner, and I was left alone for the first time in at least a week.

I went to the balcony, the blanket still wrapped around me, and sat in what had become my favorite spot. The clouds thinned, and a small patch of blue appeared above. The air instantly warmed. I stared at the park across the street and felt tears escape the corners of my eyes. I wiped them away, and the flood spilled over, blurring my view. I buried my face in my one good hand and succumbed to the emotion as it burst forth.

My whole body heaved and shuddered through the sobbing. My grief, fear, and anxiety were jumbled with my pain and relief that the demon was gone. The overwhelming mix of emotions broke down the wall I had put up years ago—every brick pulverized.

I was still crying when Jack got back. I didn't realize he was there until I felt his arms around me, his hands running over my hair.

He held me for what seemed like an eternity until I finally stopped shaking. The tears hadn't entirely stopped when I straightened to face him.

"You good?" he asked.

I nodded. "And I'm ready to talk about us."

"How about over dinner?" Jack stood and held out a hand.

I took his hand and let him gently pull me out of the chair. We wandered into the kitchen, still connected.

"I'm leaving in a few days, but I don't want to leave with questions between us," I said as we sat to eat.

"Since your apartment was totally destroyed, you're going to need a place to live. I'd like it if you'd stay at my place. I can't sell it. Not now." I took a bite of the pizza Jack had gotten and waited for his answer.

"Sure, that will give me time to find something permanent once you get back from school."

"No. Jack, I want you to live there permanently. I'm not entirely sure yet where I'm going to be after this semester."

"Liz, you admitted you still love me. I don't know why there's anything else to say. I want you in my life, and if that means I have to leave Evergreen, then I will."

"Jack, you don't need to talk me into it. I want to be with you, but I want to take it slow. I'm going to talk to Deanna about staying at her place for a while after I finish this semester. It doesn't make sense for you to leave the property if I can't stay in Evergreen. I'm going to try, but I don't want you to move unnecessarily."

"So, what made you change your mind?"

"I was already thinking about it, but now, with Shelley …" It hurt too much to say the words. "You, the brothers, and Deanna are all I have left now. I need you, all of you. I can't live the lie I was trying to make my life if I don't have Shelley. The last few weeks have made me realize the mistake I made trying to forget all of you. I won't do that again. Life's too short to hide."

Jack moved to the chair next to me and slid it right next to mine. "I'm glad to hear you say that."

# Epilogue

Dear Diary December 12, 2016.

I've kept an eye on news coming out of Evergreen since I got back to school. The fog, that mysteriously showed up just before the demon did six years ago, is gone. Not that Evergreen hasn't had any fog, but it's been the kind that you expect to see occasionally during the fall or spring, and there have been zero reports of deaths or burns attributed to it since before the night of the ritual.

Deanna's coven agrees with my theory that the fog was connected to the demon. They think it might have, in fact, been the demon's influence holding Evergreen hostage. The fog's potency diminished when we fought the demon in high school and remained relatively harmless until the demon's strength began to return.

It seems like the rest of life in Evergreen is once again quiet and unassuming, the way it should be in a small town. There have been no reports of unexplained or major incidents. The last story in the news was about a schoolteacher in Evergreen who won the Powerball jackpot.

So, this is it, my last night at Washburn. I'm going home tomorrow, to Evergreen, as someone who only left to go to university. No more hiding or running away from what scares me. Life is meant to be lived, even the scary parts, and it is way more enjoyable in the company of those who know you and still love you.

*Liz*

# About the Author

Stephanie Galay, a resident of the Okanagan Valley in British Columbia, works with numbers by day and mulls over new stories to scare people with by night. She and her husband filled the void of an empty nest with the addition of their devoted mastiff, Flower. The three of them strive to protect and adequately serve Brutus and Cesar, the two aloof but affectionate felines that rule over a large corner of their neighborhood.

Stephanie is currently working on Trapped, a supernatural homage to "Hotel California" by the Eagles, a song that has always spoken to her soul. She is also working on a trilogy under the name Bubbles and Augers.

Connect with Stephanie Galay

On Facebook: StephanieGalayAuthor
And look for me on Good Reads and BookBub.